$\mathcal{A}$ CANDLELIGHT REGENCY SPECIAL

CANDLELIGHT ROMANCES

THE RAVEN SISTERS

Dorothy Mack

A CANDLELIGHT REGENCY SPECIAL

Published by
DELL PUBLISHING CO., INC.
1 Dag Hammarskjold Plaza
New York, New York 10017

Dell ® TM 681510, Dell Publishing Co., Inc.

ISBN: 0-440-17255-1

Printed in the United States of America

First printing—July 1977

THE RAVEN SISTERS

CHAPTER 1

The antiquated traveling carriage bounded and jolted its way toward London, its passage made even more uncomfortable for the unfortunate travelers within by the deepening shadows of dusk which hindered the coachman's efforts to avoid the worst of the mud and water-filled ruts created by a two-hour cloudburst earlier in the afternoon. In an unwary moment one of the three passengers removed her hand from the strap she had been clutching with a death grip and flexed her cramped fingers briefly. It was a costly gesture, as the right front wheel descended crazily into a particularly pernicious depression, throwing her sharply against the door. Her very fetching sapphire blue bonnet departed from its fashionable angle atop her shining curls to perch recklessly over one eye. A small grimace of pain marred her beautiful countenance for an instant, and as she rubbed the shoulder that had taken the shock of the jolt, she was betrayed into a quite uncharacteristic acidity:

"If Papa bore us the least affection he would have this horrid chaise resprung. It is beyond my understanding how Aunt can sleep through all this bouncing and jerking."

The eyes of the even younger lady sitting opposite the speaker and next to an older woman of ample proportions gleamed with amusement as she watched her sister's attempts to retie her bonnet while maintaining a somewhat precarious balance. Her voice, though, held a wry note.

"Perhaps it is because she is leaning on me—crushingly so—and I am absorbing the greater portion of the jolting for her. Pray do not wake her though, Liza, for then we should have to endure her moaning and complaining about the discomfort and I would very likely have to hold her vinaigrette constantly to her nose. I much prefer her weight." Her voice changed to mock severity: "And as for your first statement, I never heard anything more hen-witted. You know very well Papa does not care a scrap for either of us. He has never forgiven *me* for not being born a boy, and although your resemblance to Mama may have made you tolerably pleasing to him in the past—when he ever spared you a thought, that is—ever since Grandfather died and made you his heiress, you have become a constant source of annoyance to him. Especially since your trustees make sure Papa cannot get his hands on your fortune, which was a very wise move on Grandfather's part to be sure, for you know Papa would only gamble it away. If he had to be a gamester why could he not have been a lucky gamester? Just look at these dowdy clothes I am wearing," she uttered in despairing accents, casting a look of extreme loathing over the heavy brown cloak that overpowered her diminutive figure.

"Oh, Carina, Dearest, you must not speak so disrespectfully of poor Papa," Miss Elizabeth

Raven interpolated hurriedly before her disgusted sister could further elaborate. "Indeed if Aunt were to hear you she would give you a terrible scold. It is most unseemly. I . . . I know Papa's is not a particularly demonstrative nature, but it is unjust to assume he does not feel toward us all the affection natural to a parent." Catching her sister's sardonic glance she trailed off into silence.

"Oh, pooh, do not talk such fustian to me. I hope I know better than to discuss Papa before others but between ourselves there should be no lies. When did he ever treat us with anything but complete indifference? As far as I have been able to observe, all Papa's actions are motivated by his own interests or pleasures. And what was in that letter from him this morning that sent us down to Ravenshill posthaste? Why were you alone with Papa for hours? With Aunt Augusta in constant attendance, I have not been able to question you until now, but you were looking worried earlier. Has Papa reneged on his agreement to attend my ball after all? I promise you I shan't repine if we have to cancel it. It was all your idea that I make my come-out you know, Liza. I was perfectly happy to remain at Ravenshill where I could ride every day. And the squire would have allowed me to hunt with his pack this year."

"Carina, I could not leave you alone at Ravenshill again this season while I enjoyed myself in Society. Now that I have the income from Grandfather's legacy, I can supply you with a suitable wardrobe." As her sister's face took on a familiar mulish look she added hastily, "Yes, I know it is Papa's duty to underwrite your debut, but the truth is that the cards have been running very badly just lately and when that wretched horse Papa backed at Newmarket stumbled at the post he was left in a precarious position. I am persuaded it is only a temporary setback and he will soon make a recovery, but you are almost eighteen, Dearest, and it is time you made your curtsy to society. And you know that I am turned twenty, almost on the shelf. I must make a push to establish myself and I cannot leave you alone at Ravenshill to run wild like a boy."

Carina, who had been staring at her unusually loquacious sister with uncomfortable intensity, now broke in: "If you think to divert me with nonsensical talk about being on the shelf, you are indeed a ninnyhammer, Liza. You are by far the most beautiful girl in London, and even if you were over thirty and a positive antidote, Grandfather's ninety thousand pounds would make you one of the catches of this or any season. Why did Papa wish to see you today? We have been in London for almost a fortnight and he has not bothered to send us so much as a greeting before. Did he try to get money out of you?"

As her sister hesitated momentarily, she declared suspiciously, "Liza, did Papa threaten not to appear at my ball unless you settled his debts?"

"No, of course not," Elizabeth stammered, grateful that the deepening dusk hid her heated cheeks from her sister's sharp eyes. "Papa simply wished to discuss some details of the arrangements with me and his gout prevented him from coming to us."

Carina, whose intelligence was no less acute than her eyesight, remained unconvinced by the gentle Elizabeth's attempt at a setdown, but at that moment a particularly violent jolting of the carriage caused their Aunt Augusta to moan slightly and launch herself immediately into a querulous monologue, bewailing in tragic accents a malign fate that had at once thrust her into a contraption fit only for a torture chamber and cast her upon the nonexistent mercies of a brother-in-law who was ever a monster of selfishness and two irresponsible girls with no more sense than to undertake a journey on a day when any fool could see it was bound to come on to rain, and all for a whim, or at least for no intelligent purpose that had been confided to *her*.

The two girls, correctly interpreting this complaint as due to pique at not being informed of the context of the private conversation between Elizabeth and her father at Ravenshill, set out at once to soothe the ruffled feathers of their relative.

It could not be denied that Augusta Silverdown was more good-natured than intelligent, being a foolish woman addicted to gossip and often a prey to purely imaginary ailments, but she had been the only maternal figure the two girls had known since their mother's death some eight years previously. Out of a genuine love for her sister's children, she more or less patiently endured the unconcealed contempt of a brother-in-law whose manners had never been conciliatory even when the wife he loved fiercely had been alive to act as a buffer between him and his in-laws. Elizabeth and Carina were not blind to her faults but loved her dearly for her undoubted kindness in sacrificing for years her own inclinations for the social life in order to care for her nieces in the country.

Now they bent their best efforts toward sooth-

ing this current *crise de nerfs* that had left their
aunt moaning about a violent headache due to
the jolting of the chaise. To this end Carina
gently removed the reticule from her compul-
sive clutch and searched for the ever-present
vinaigrette while Elizabeth embarked on an involved, and for the most part untruthful, explanation of their journey to Ravenshill at their father's
request. During the better portion of this highly
colored account, Miss Silverdown heard her out in
unresponsive silence. She ventured no comment
on her brother-in-law's alleged interest in the
guest list and decor proposed for Carina's ball,
nor did she cavil at the highly unlikely picture of
his actually submitting suggestions for the menu
and offering to select the wines, but when Elizabeth, emboldened by this promising reception, became so carried away by her own eloquence as to
imply that Papa had been so beset by the low
spirits attendant on an attack of gout as to desire
the company of his dear daughters, she roused
herself enough to give a snort of disgust which
fortunately drowned out the choke of laughter
Carina was struggling to turn into a cough.

"Ha! If he was so desirous of your company
what prevented him from insisting on our spending the night at Ravenshill when that cloudburst
delayed our return to town? Look at that sky! I
shall deem myself fortunate indeed to escape a
broken axle or even worse at this time of day. And
to allow us to leave without even the escort of a
stable boy is all of a piece with his lack of consideration. Much good John Coachman would be
to us in an emergency. I should be hard put to be-

lieve he is a day less than sixty and I daresay has
not so much as a horse pistol with him either."

Carina, who had been peering out into the
deepening gloom during this speech, remarked
cheerfully: "Do not agitate yourself, Aunt, we
shall be home shortly. See, we are already crossing Hounslow Heath."

Just at that moment a deeper shadow separated
itself from a clump of trees about a hundred feet
ahead and rode into the path of the oncoming
carriage. A shot rang out, then a shouted command. Carina, who had been looking out of the
window, was the only passenger who had time to
brace herself against the sudden reining in of the
horses. Elizabeth's hat again descended over her
eye as she was thrown with some force against the
far side door. Miss Silverdown suffered a similar
indignity. Before either could give utterance to
her surprise, the door was jerked open and a
rough voice demanded that they get out and
"step lively" while obeying the order.

Elizabeth got down first and assisted her
greatly flustered aunt to descend from the carriage. In the brief interval allowed her, Carina,
frantically searching for a weapon, seized upon
her aunt's umbrella as the only item that might
prove useful and, concealing it under her cloak,
jumped down to join her frightened relatives. She
saw with faint relief that only a single highwayman, now dismounted, confronted them; but as
he was possessed of two pistols, one in his hand
pointed at John Coachman and one stuck in his
belt while they were completely unarmed, the
fact of their numerical superiority could scarcely
be said to increase their chances of emerging from

the incident in full possession of their valuables. Her stupid brain refused to come up with a single useful suggestion to avert disaster and she went to stand where the robber indicated with outward meekness.

He snorted with contempt at the meager hoard of coins disgorged from John Coachman's pockets and commanded the women to strip off their gloves and hand over all their jewelry while he grabbed the reticule from Miss Silverdown himself and began turning out its contents, carelessly dropping her handkerchief, small scissors and other miscellaneous articles to the ground. Seizing a small wad of bank notes, he stuffed them into a pocket of his greatcoat and discarded the reticule. He dismissed Carina with a sharp glance which took in all of her small, heavily covered figure, noting the complete absence of rings or other jewelry. She held her breath that the umbrella she had left leaning against her leg under the cloak while she complied with the order to remove her gloves would not fall to the ground before his raking eyes passed over her, and in this luck favored her so she was able to grasp it again by withdrawing her hand under the cloak. Her quick ears had caught the sound of hoofbeats approaching and she was scarcely able to breathe with mingled fear and anticipation.

The highwayman, in the act of demanding Elizabeth's reticule, became aware of the approach of a horseman too and jerked his head in the direction of the sounds. In that instant Carina acted. Pushing apart the front of her cloak, she raised the folded umbrella with both hands and brought it down across the thief's outstretched arms with all the force of which she was capable, knocking the pistol from his hand. Before he could move to recover it the oncoming rider reined in quickly, shouting:

"Don't move a muscle unless you wish a bullet between your eyes!"

Carina did not await a formal suggestion on the part of their rescuer to dart forward and retrieve the highwayman's fallen pistol which she immediately handed to the coachman.

"If you would be so good as to remove the other weapon from his belt, ma'am," requested the still-mounted stranger politely of Elizabeth, though his eyes never left the masked and greatcoated figure now standing rigid with fury.

Elizabeth drew back with involuntary distaste and Carina moved forward to perform this action. She did not need the stranger's sharp command to avoid getting between him and the thief, but quickly seized the spent pistol, glancing straightly at the unsuccessful robber as she did so. The mask covering the upper part of his face prevented her from forming a complete picture of his countenance, but she was quick to note a long scar running from the left side of his nose almost underneath his chin. His eyes glittered behind the slits of his mask as he returned her stare, and he said softly for her ears only:

"I'll remember you again, too, missy."

Carina shivered slightly at the menace in the hissed words and drew back, trying to conceal her perturbation that he had discerned her thoughts.

"Good girl," said their rescuer briefly. He had dismounted by this time and coolly demanded that the would-be thief return everything he had taken.

John Coachman poked him sharply with his own pistol to hasten the operation and took the coins and notes reluctantly removed from the huge pockets in the man's greatcoat.

While this was being accomplished in complete silence on the part of the thief, Miss Silverdown, who had been keening softly to herself since watching her reticule emptied, began to give vent to a continually rising hysteria. Elizabeth was trying vainly to soothe her and Carina tried to assist by scrambling in the semidarkness to recover her discarded possessions. For a second the stranger seemed at a loss, then with a command to the coachman to watch the prisoner, he approached the two women hesitantly and was just in time to catch the sagging form of the elder as she gave way to her emotions and collapsed into his arms.

"Oh, Aunt, please do not," Elizabeth begged, nearly in tears herself.

Carina, approaching with the refilled reticule, was unable to suppress a smile of pure amusement as she glimpsed the strange young man's expression. He was staring at Elizabeth over the inert form of her aunt and he looked as stunned as a man who has just felt a bullet whiz past his head. Carina, used to observing her beautiful sister's effect on susceptible males, said calmly, "Let me help you get her into the coach, sir, before we revive her and before you sink under her weight." She strove to present a bland countenance, but their rescuer had caught the amusement in her voice, and guessing its cause, his own response was rather stiff.

"Of course. If you will just open the door, child, and climb in, I will hand her up to you."

Carina mounted the steps quickly and helped the man gently settle his burden onto the seat. "Leave her to me," she said abruptly and he backed out again. He had just removed his hat and was making his bow to Elizabeth when the sound of hoofbeats near at hand caused him to jerk his head up, a thunderous expression on his face. He whirled around and started to run to his horse but was arrested in flight by Elizabeth's urgent cry:

"He has hurt John Coachman! Please help me."

The young man gave his horse one disgusted slap and muttered something in Basic English under his breath before loping toward the front of the carriage where Elizabeth was attempting to assist the old coachman to rise to a sitting position. He groaned and raised a shaking hand to the back of his neck. After a moment when his head became clearer, he accepted the offer of a strong arm to aid him onto his feet, meeting the young man's eyes with a shamed expression in his own.

"I'm that sorry to let you down, sir. It was the horses moving a bit restless like that distracted me. When I turned my head he hit me in the neck and made off as quick as you please, the sneak."

"Never mind," said the stranger brusquely. "I should have grabbed his horse before dismounting myself. My wits were wandering with everything happening so fast. Will you be able to drive?"

"Oh, I'll be fit as a trivet in a moment, sir," said the coachman gratefully, and added with grim satisfaction, "At least he didn't get away with anything, including his own pistols, but it would have given me great pleasure to deposit him in Bow Street, it would."

Elizabeth's sweet voice intervened, "Thank goodness you are all right, John. Do not blame yourself because the thief escaped. If Aunt had not swooned you would have had your prisoner." Turning to the stranger she said with charming sincerity, "Thank you so very much, sir, for coming to our aid so gallantly. We are indeed most grateful and my aunt will wish to thank you personally when she has made a recovery."

Again the young man swept off his curly brimmed beaver and made her a bow. "Permit me to introduce myself, ma'am. I am Gavin Delawney, very much at your service. I only regret that my aid was of such a trifling nature and that we shall not now be able to bring that fellow before a magistrate."

"Oh, pray do not tease yourself about that, sir. I promise you my aunt and sister and I are vastly relieved to have escaped with our belongings intact. My name is Elizabeth Raven. My aunt, Miss Silverdown, my sister, Carina, and I were returning to town from our home, Ravenshill, when we were stopped."

"I am delighted to make your acquaintance, Miss Raven, and beg you will accept my escort for the remainder of your journey."

"Oh, thank you, sir. It is very good of you to offer, and this will surely help restore Aunt Augusta's spirits. I must see how she does. Do you care to come and meet her?" she asked hesitantly, not wishing to delay their start, for it was now quite dark and the coachman would be growing impatient.

Gavin, who would have agreed to meet the devil himself in company with the most beautiful girl he had ever set eyes on, assented readily and followed her to the carriage, where he assisted her to enter. Inside, Carina had succeeded in restoring her aunt to a semblance of normalcy but, knowing that very susceptible lady would have succumbed to another attack of nerves if left alone, she was unable to satisfy her curiosity as to what was taking place outside and was awaiting her sister in a fever of impatience. She too had heard the sound of hoofbeats but the darkness prevented her from seeing whether the thief had been recaptured.

Elizabeth was much relieved to see her aunt's composure restored and begged leave to present their rescuer who now entered the carriage behind her. Miss Silverdown greeted him effusively and thanked him so warmly that he grew embarrassed and was almost relieved when a singularly lovely voice interrupted, saying with a hint of censure, "So he got away after all?"

"I am afraid so, Miss ahh . . ."

"Carina," said the voice, adding philosophically, "Ah well, I suppose you could not have been supporting Aunt and tying up a thief at the same time. A pity though."

Gavin realized with wry humor that, although two of the ladies were overflowing with gratitude toward him, the third was having to bite her tongue to avoid censure for a job half done. He said with mock humility, "I sincerely beg your pardon for bungling the capture, Miss Carina, but

I think I would know him again so perhaps I shall have the opportunity to seize him for you yet."

"Perhaps. It is not very likely though," came the somewhat wistful reply.

Bloodthirsty little wretch, thought Gavin humorously.

The other two ladies combined to reprove her gently for her ungraciousness to their gallant rescuer.

"Ah, no," he intervened hastily, "the child is absolutely correct and what is more it was she who disarmed the thief by that rather unorthodox though very effective method, so she must be allowed her very natural regret at seeing her handiwork go for naught."

"Very prettily said," approved the voice from the other side of the carriage, "and of course I am most grateful to you for arriving in the nick of time just like the heroes in the novels we get from Hookham's."

By this time Gavin was most desirous to see the owner of that mischievous voice in good light, but conditions made that an impossible wish for the moment so he repeated his offer to escort them home and, after promising to call on the morrow to see how they did, politely took his leave of them and signaled to the coachman to resume their journey.

CHAPTER 2

Less than an hour later Mr. Gavin Delawney entered his own house in Cavendish Square after taking immediate leave of his new acquaintances as they drew up outside their Green Street residence. He had had time on the ride back to London to remember that he was playing host to a friend that evening so must curb his impatience to further his acquaintance with the beautiful Miss Raven. Still her image filled his mind as he stripped off his gloves of York tan and absent-mindedly tossed hat and greatcoat to the porter.

"Sir Edward Lynton is in the book room, sir," announced that individual.

"What, already? Thank you, Matthew. Tell them to delay dinner thirty minutes." He gave one quick tug at his neckcloth before entering the book room swiftly.

"Hullo, Ned. Sorry to be late. I hope my people looked after you all right?" He nodded with satisfaction as the large man lounging comfortably in a wing chair by a roaring fire smiled lazily and lifted a glass of Madeira in response.

Gavin crossed to the fireplace and allowed the heat to waft over him briefly. "Ah, that feels good. No one riding on the Knightsbridge Road at six this evening would believe it is already mid-April. Felt more like January."

"May one inquire why you were on the Knightsbridge Road this evening when you'd lured me here with promises of lobster *à la François?*"

"I'd been down at Blowton Hall with Corny for a few days and decided to ride back, so I sent Finkston ahead with the curricle. Got held up—literally. You'll get your lobster in due course. If you'll pour me a glass of that Madeira you may accompany me upstairs while I change and regale you with a tale of an angel and a rescue."

"You intrigue me," said his friend following him up to his bedchamber. "Did heavenly protection fail then? Was this angel in need of rescue?"

Sir Edward dropped into a chair and placed Mr. Delawney's glass on a small table while that individual pulled the cord summoning his valet. He smiled indulgently at the eager expression on the younger man's face. At thirty Edward felt much older than the four years seniority that actually existed between the friends. The two men had not known each other at school because of the gap but had become firm friends since first meeting at Jackson's Boxing Saloon two years before. Sir Edward, taller and broader than Gavin and considered an excellent exponent of the art of boxing, had been singularly impressed by the speed, insouciance and sheer science of the other's style, and he readily acknowledged the explosive power of his right hand. Of very dissimilar character, the two contrived to enjoy each other's company nonetheless.

Edward, who stood over six feet tall and was

powerfully built, gave an impression of great strength at all times under strict control. His very regular features, though most pleasing, were habitually cast in a rather grave expression, and his slow speech and lazy manner contributed to this impression of quiet strength. His coloring was unremarkable, hair medium brown and eyes of an indeterminate hazel. One might be tempted to attribute to him a cold disposition unless one had been privileged to witness the transformation wrought by his rare smile, enlivening those grave eyes and irradiating all within its range by the warmth and kindness thus revealed.

In contrast to Sir Edward, Gavin was of medium height, lean and wiry, with a feline grace and surging vitality. His coloring was most remarkable, the dark red hair almost startling in its vibrancy, paired with eyes of a blazing blue. Extraordinarily white teeth gleamed in a compelling smile that urged the world to participate in the sheer excitement of living. At the age of six and twenty he was still discovering new adventures and was unacquainted with the chastening effect of failure or disappointment. His was the irrestible force that made things happen.

At that moment he was engaged in ripping his cravat from his throat with one hand while holding the glass to his lips with the other. He grinned at his friend's mildly expressed curiosity.

"You might say I rescued the angel—she says so, bless her—but the truth is I did no such thing. It was just my good fortune to appear at the crucial moment."

"Would it inconvenience you greatly to tell the story as it happened for the benefit of a more prosaic mind? You might begin with the angel's identity—I trust you had the wit to learn her name?"

"Her name is Elizabeth Raven, but instead of being dark as the name implies, she is angelically fair and unbelievably beautiful." Gavin stopped his panegyric for a moment devoted to the delighted recollection of Miss Elizabeth Raven's smile. He was unaware of the sudden tension in the other man's bearing.

Sir Edward said carefully, "I know just how beautiful she is. I have been acquainted with Elizabeth all her life. I trust she was not hurt?"

It was the younger man's turn to show surprise. "What, are you acquainted with the Ravens? Why have you not told me? Why have I never heard of her before? A diamond like this one cannot live in obscurity, surely?"

"Elizabeth was presented last year, but before the season was a month old she removed to Ravenshill to be with her sister who had contracted a severe case of influenza. They are very devoted. Even in the short time she was in town she had several offers, I believe. She is also an heiress," he finished shortly.

"If she hadn't a groat she would have offers," declared Gavin roundly. "The girl is magnificent."

"I would not think of disagreeing with you. What happened this evening? I was unaware the Ravens were in town."

"Miss Raven said they were on their way back to town from Ravenshill, she and her sister and an aunt who had hysterics all over the place, when they were stopped by a highwayman on Hounslow Heath. I heard a shot and galloped up to the scene in time to prevent the robbery. Not that

I did anything, mind you; the girl knocked the pistol out of the thief's hand when he turned toward me. Fortunately he was alone."

"*Elizabeth* disarmed a thief? Good God!" Sir Edward's tone was eloquent of disbelief.

"No, no, that was the other one, a little dab of a schoolgirl. She cracked an umbrella across his arm." He chuckled reminiscently.

"Carina isn't a schoolgirl though I agree she is tiny. Yes, I can see Carina coolly striking a blow given the opportunity. She always ran wild at Ravenshill. Matthew Raven wanted a son and unfortunately Carina has tried to be that son. Elizabeth will have her hands full if she means to bring her sister out this season."

"Never mind the sister," said Gavin impatiently.

"You would not say that if you knew Carina," was the calm reply. "Did you not get a good look at her, then?"

"Well, no, but I cannot credit that anyone could be as beautiful as Elizabeth. Such eyes, such glowing skin, and that hair like new-minted guineas ..."

"Ah, yes, Elizabeth is indeed as beautiful a girl as any man could desire. In time Carina will be just as lovely in a different style—the two girls are not at all alike, you know, but at no time can Carina be ignored. I repeat, Elizabeth will find herself sorely tried if she hopes to turn Carina into a model debutante."

Gavin glanced across from the dressing table, where he was furiously brushing his hair, to see a faintly enigmatic expression on the older man's face. "Good heavens, if the girl has so little conduct she is better left in the country," he declared callously.

"I would not let any such hint escape my lips if I were intent on furthering my acquaintance with Elizabeth," said Edward dryly. "Carina is a rogue, but an enchanting rogue for all that, and Elizabeth is deeply attached to her."

"I am grateful for your wise counsel, my dear Ned. I can see that Miss Carina and I shall become fast friends."

The thought that Edward might himself be rather deeply attached to the owner of the mischievous voice crossed Gavin's mind fleetingly, only to be dismissed. She was obviously a child and his friend was a man of thirty years and sober habits. He allowed his valet to assist him into a coat of black superfine and accepted from him a single ruby for his cravat and a gold fob for his vest, waving the good man aside when he attemped to persuade him to don a large ruby ring. He slipped an enameled snuffbox into his pocket and bowed his friend through the door.

On the way down the marble staircase, Edward said, "What happened to the thief? Did you deliver him to Bow Street?"

"No, unfortunately he got away. The aunt had hysterics and swooned in my arms and while I was getting her into the carriage he turned on the old coachman and escaped on his horse."

Edward paused on the stairs frowning slightly, but all he said was, "Unfortunate."

Gavin flushed slightly. "Yes, I know I should have tied his horse to the chaise but it all happened so quickly, and I was rather occupied with Miss Silverdown. The girl thought I might have handled the affair rather more neatly also," he added, laughing shortly.

For the first time real amusement crept into Edward's eyes. "Carina? Yes I daresay she was disappointed to lose her prisoner. Well, my friend, produce that lobster. I have waited long enough."

Miss Carina Raven knocked peremptorily on the door to her sister's bedchamber, then entered impetuously without waiting for permission.

"Look at me, Liza, just bursting out of this dress. I cannot go into company looking like this— it . . . it is positively indecent! Aunt will have to hold me excused when Mr. Delawney calls this morning."

Elizabeth was sitting at a satinwood dressing table while Abby, the girl who waited on the sisters, dressed her hair in a simple style, threading a red ribbon through the golden curls. She was wearing a charming red woolen dress with long sleeves and a yoke of Venetian lace, presenting an altogether delightful appearance. Her sweetly serious expression was replaced by a rare mischievous smile as her glance surveyed her sister in the blue jersey dress that was obviously not in its first or even second season and quickly returned to the woebegone countenance.

"You do look a proper waif, Dearest," she agreed readily, "but we can at least be grateful you have finally developed some feminine curves. A year ago one could not tell you from a thirteen-year-old boy."

Carina grinned suddenly, saucily, increasing for an instant her resemblance to a thirteen-year-old boy: "True, but I shall postpone my gratitude until my new clothes arrive, for I am a prisoner in this house in the meantime."

"That is why I have persuaded Aunt to deny us to any callers this past week. There was so much to do to prepare for your ball. Cheer up, the gowns will be here any day now, and there is no certainty that Mr. Delawney will call today, you know. His manners are so polished he probably felt he must express his intention to call to see how we did. Very likely it has already slipped his mind."

Carina stared at her sister, wondering for the hundredth time how she contrived to remain totally unaware of the effect she had on most men, but she merely said dryly, "I wish I were as certain of heaven as I am that we shall receive a morning visit from Mr. Gavin Delawney. If that gentleman does not intend to pursue his acquaintance, nay his advantage, with you then you may call me the greatest goosecap in London."

"Well, I am sure we shall all be delighted to receive Mr. Delawney when he calls, for indeed we owe him a debt of gratitude. I hold that it is not certain he will call today, but what to do if he does? You cannot appear in that ill-fitting gown, Carina."

"That is what I have been telling you these last ten minutes. You will have to present my excuses."

"Miss Carina," broke in the abigail at this point, "I have been trying to tell you, two of your dresses were delivered yesterday while you were away. I put them in your wardrobe."

"Good heavens! How could they have escaped my notice? Oh, of course, you had laid this gown over a chair, Abby. Are you finished here? Will you come help me decide which to wear?" She was already through the door on the words.

The maid looked questioningly at Elizabeth who smiled and said, "Wait for me; I am coming too."

In her room Carina had already unfastened her dress and was stepping out of it. She held it out to the maid.

"Burn it," she said cheerfully to Abby, "and all the others too unless you know someone even smaller than I who might wear them."

"Oh, yes, miss," breathed the abigail ecstatically, "my two younger sisters would be thrilled to have them. One is fourteen and t'other is almost twelve. My mother and I will make them fit. Thank you ever so much, Miss Carina." Her hands were shaking with excitement as she gently lifted the first of the new gowns over her mistress's head and began to do up the buttons.

"Ooh, it feels so smooth," crooned Carina, luxuriating in soft featherweight wool which fell in graceful folds to her feet. She twisted impatiently to catch a glimpse of herself in the pier glass over the dressing table.

"Do stand still, Miss Carina," begged the little maid, "or I'll never get these buttons fastened." Her skillful fingers accomplished the task despite her mistress's twisting and turning. "There you are. I declare you look a picture in that deep green color, miss." Abby's eyes were full of honest admiration as she gazed at the transformation wrought by a well-cut and perfectly fitted garment in the appearance of the previously insignificant figure of the younger sister. Of course Miss Elizabeth was a real beauty, but when Miss Carina was sparkling with delight as she was now, it was hard to take one's eyes off her.

"Yes, you really look lovely in that color, Carina," said Elizabeth, rising from the chair where she had been indulgently watching her sister's excited behavior. "Turn slowly and walk away from me. Oh, yes, Céleste has done a marvelous job. The length and fit are perfect and I do believe, Dearest, that that plain, high-waisted style makes you appear taller. Do you not agree, Abby?"

"Oh, yes, miss," confirmed the maid.

Carina's eyes were dancing with impish delight as she swept them both an exaggerated curtsy.

"You are too kind, mademoiselles. Nothing can make the runt of the litter appear tall I fear, but I do think I look rather nice," she added with innocent vanity. "It is so wonderful to have new clothes finally." She threw her arms about her startled sister and hugged her almost fiercely. "You are so good to me, Liza. I shall really try to be a credit to you. If only I can remember to keep my lips sealed until I have thought whether what I am about to utter is a fitting sentiment for a young lady in society to express."

Elizabeth laughed at the slight pucker of anxiety between her sister's well-shaped black brows. "You do not look too hopeful. I have more confidence in your natural instincts for what is fitting, Carina. Now let us see how the yellow gown becomes you."

Carina obediently stood still while Abby tenderly removed the emerald gown and substituted a daffodil yellow muslin confection. She still looked a little subdued, however, and confessed breathlessly, "Yes, but, Liza, I am afraid very often I do not wish to do what is fitting. So much of one's social behavior is simply the most blatant hypocrisy. 'How well you look today, my dear, I declare that gown takes ten years from your age,'" she mimicked in an affected tone, "when all the time one is thinking with positively ghoulish pleasure how foolish a plump matron looks in a young girl's dress."

Elizabeth said with her usual calm good sense, "You may refrain from offering insincere compliments with my blessing, my dear, as long as you have the good manners and consideration not to utter wounding truths in their stead. Social intercourse is to a certain extent an artificial experience, but that is the way matters stand. I shall certainly help you to avoid awkward situations. Ah," she added in a satisfied tone, "this too was a wise decision. With your dramatic coloring you must always choose vibrant shades, Carina, and avoid the pale pastels even though they are popular."

"I wish I could wear simply any color as you can, Liza," said her sister somewhat wistfully, "especially red. How I hate my hair!"

"Don't be nonsensical," came the prompt retort. "I am persuaded your hair will have many admirers. No one can say you are in the common style. I have never seen such rich, dark red hair on anyone before; even Papa's was not so deep. It is perfectly beautiful with your creamy complexion. You are indeed fortunate to have escaped the pale skin and freckles which usually detract from red hair."

"Nevertheless I hate it. It is too long and heavy

and far too curly to be trained in the current styles."

"Untamed like you, Dearest," agreed Elizabeth with a rueful smile in her beautiful harebell eyes. "We will put you in Alexandre's hands before your ball. Why not tie it back for now and decide which dress you will wear this morning? Aunt Augusta will be wondering why we are keeping to our rooms so long."

Since the house, though rather shabby from neglect since Mrs. Raven's death, was comfortably heated, Carina decided to keep on the yellow dress and presently the two girls, as blooming as the first red and yellow tulips of spring, descended the stairs happily.

Miss Silverdown, encountered in the yellow saloon giving a final touch to an arrangement of spring flowers, was quick to applaud the improvement in her young niece's appearance but ended her praise on a slightly chastening note:

"Now if only I could be as sure that your behavior will be conformable, I could really look forward to this season. It has been such a long time since I have seen much of my oldest friends. Last year we had barely settled here before we hurried back to Ravenshill."

"I know—to nurse me," Carina said contritely. "Poor Liza has not really had her first season yet and now she has to watch over me."

"Nonsense," her sister returned briskly. "I have every expectation of enjoying myself immensely, much more so with you than without you. At least life is never dull when you are around."

Carina glanced at her sister quickly but could detect nothing significant in the serene coun-

tenance. Liza had seemed slightly different in the
past two years, more subdued, less eager for each
new experience than in the past, with a calm acceptance of everything that happened. Remembering with nostalgia the laughing, expectant girl
who joined in her sister's less riotous explorations
and follies, she wondered, not for the first time, if
the change in Liza was more than a natural sobering as she left girlhood behind. Had anything
happened to bring about this banking down of
the fires? Would she not have told her sister if
there was some shadow over her life? She dismissed her wandering thoughts impatiently. She
was growing fanciful. Liza certainly never gave
the impression of sadness concealed, but there
was a disturbingly mysterious quality about her
smile at times as if her thoughts were elsewhere.
Well, now that she herself was in London too she
would be in a better position to observe her sister.

The ladies had seated themselves with their
sewing when Miss Silverdown discovered to her
considerable annoyance that her favorite thimble
was missing. The sisters were quite accustomed to
their aunt's propensity for mislaying her belongings and Carina cheerfully offered to go in search
of it. She got up with alacrity, pleased with any
excuse to lay down her embroidery, a task that
never appealed since it could only be accomplished in a sitting position. It was a fine, clear
morning after yesterday's rain and she yearned to
be on a horse cantering in the park since there
was little probability of a gallop in the country.
She devoutly hoped her new riding habit would
be the next garment to arrive. The inactivity of
town dwelling was beginning to chafe, but she

had promised Liza to try to conform to the pattern of a debutante and she was determined not to spoil her sister's pleasure in having her with her in London. Liza was so used to looking after her that she would have sacrificed her own season to remain at Ravenshill had Carina not seemed willing to come to town. She slowly mounted the stairs to her aunt's bedchamber and enlisted the help of one of the maids in searching for the elusive silver thimble. It was immediately located in a small workbasket in her aunt's dressing room, but she lingered in conversation with the maid, a country girl who missed the greater freedom of movement associated with country living.

Her aunt's voice drifted out to her as she approached the yellow saloon quite twenty minutes later, and something in the unusual animation in its tones warned Carina that they had a visitor. Casting a hasty glance in a pier glass in the hall, she reassured herself that with the exception of her deplorable hair she was looking her best. She entered the room with a new confidence born of this satisfaction and smilingly approached the trio seated on the straw-colored satin chairs grouped near the fireplace. She had been instantly aware of the identity of the gentleman who had risen to his feet at her entrance, and she flashed her sister a triumphant glance which Elizabeth blandly ignored. Mr. Delawney, however, intercepted the look and had no hesitation in translating "I told you so." His eyes narrowed just slightly, but he smiled charmingly at Carina and came forward to take her hand. As he did so his coat brushed lightly against the worktable beside Miss Silverdown's chair, dislodging a small pair of scissors which fell to the carpet near Carina's feet. Both Carina and Gavin bent simultaneously to retrieve them and her head came into abrupt contact with his chin. She was off balance and therefore grateful for the hand which seized her arm and steadied her as they both rose, he with the scissors in his other hand. Carina raised a ruefully smiling countenance to his but what she saw caused her smile to freeze slightly and her eyes to widen in astonishment.

Gavin too was staring at her while little ripples ran along his nerves. Ned had been quite correct after all—this one was a beauty too—or would be when she grew up, he amended, recalling the mischief he had noted in her voice on the previous day and in her eyes an instant ago. Those eyes held his attention now; large and expressive, they dominated her small, oval face. They were a curious light gray, but the irises were ringed with a deeper color at the perimeter, almost as though outlined in ink, he mused. The quite startling effect was further enhanced by preposterously long curling eyelashes of jet black. He wondered fleetingly if the minx darkened them till common sense reasserted itself; of course her aunt would never permit such a thing.

None of this startled conjecturing was revealed on his face. Except for the narrowing of those brilliant blue eyes, his expression was merely politely regretful as he murmured a conventional apology for their collision.

That Carina experienced no such reticence was immediately apparent. She was still staring at him wide-eyed.

"Good heaven," she uttered at last, "your hair—

it is exactly the same color as mine." Then turning abruptly to her aunt: "We could be brother and sister. Are you quite certain Papa has not been concealing a brother from us all these years?" she inquired with real interest.

"Carina! Dearest!" breathed Elizabeth in horror while their aunt, for once stricken to speechlessness, turned a mottled shade of crimson and opened and shut her mouth spasmodically.

Into the breach came a gust of hearty masculine laughter:

"Unless your father happened to be in Italy twenty-six years ago, I think we must not accuse my mother of playing my father false but rather accept coincidence as the explanation for this unusual circumstance," he replied with commendable composure.

Before Miss Silverdown could dwell further upon the extremely improper turn the conversation had taken with the entrance of her younger niece, which fact was still having a paralyzing effect on her vocal cords, their guest proceeded to conduct Carina to a chair, remarking smoothly:

"I have never until this minute admired the color of my hair, Miss Carina, but that is all in the past. I am proud to share a trait with a remarkably lovely lady."

If he hoped to disconcert the young girl with such pointed gallantry, he failed completely in his object, for Carina turned the compliment aside summarily.

"Pooh, nonsense! The sole advantage in having hair this awful color was that it was thought to be unique. Now neither of us can any longer claim such exclusiveness. And," she added wistfully, "I should have liked to have a brother."

Here Elizabeth plunged in to switch the conversation to safer channels. Although he abetted her efforts admirably, Gavin's thoughts lingered on the redheaded girl sitting opposite him for a moment longer. She need not have feared to lose her claim to uniqueness, he reflected between amusement and censure. Certainly in his experience he had not come across such an unself-conscious young girl. She seemed alike immune to blushing and averse to compliments, and in addition possessed a tongue which would land her in disgrace unless he missed his guess. A really abominable brat. Ned had been correct also in his assumption that launching this one would prove a hazardous task for her sister and aunt.

Elizabeth was explaining that they had only come up to London quite recently and were still living quietly while preparing for Carina's ball.

"The invitations have already gone out but we would be delighted if you would join us then." She paused, smiling at Gavin, and he was convinced there was no more beautiful sight in London than Miss Elizabeth Raven's smile.

"Most assuredly I will come," he smiled back, ruthlessly canceling out any previous engagements in his mind. "It will be a great pleasure to help launch Miss Carina," he continued smoothly.

There was nothing in his voice to object to and he had not taken his eyes from Elizabeth's face, but Carina felt sure he was mocking her and raised her slightly pointed little chin a trifle as she accepted the challenge with alacrity:

"Perhaps I should extort a promise from you

now to dance with me to assure that I am not a
wallflower at my own ball," she suggested with
suspicious sweetness.

Elizabeth laughed, her aunt clucked reprov-
ingly, but The Enemy, as Carina had already
mentally dubbed this maddeningly assured man,
merely bowed with effortless grace, saying, "I
predict that I shall have to fight my way forward
to come within asking distance that night so I
shall promptly accept your kind offer to dance,
Miss Carina. And may I also be assured of the
pleasure of a dance with you, Miss Raven?" he
asked, dismissing Carina's gaucherie and turning
his attention once more to Elizabeth.

She assented readily and he prepared to take
his departure, pausing only to invite the ladies to
drive out with him the following afternoon. Miss
Silverdown declined due to a prior engagement
but assured him the girls would be delighted to
accept. Elizabeth assented with pleasure and Gavin glanced at Carina to encounter a speculative
gleam in the cool gray eyes. He awaited her next
move with concealed amusement.

Carina was thinking that she might as well
make use of this latest of Elizabeth's conquests.
"Is your offer open to negotiation?" she inquired
politely.

Gavin grinned. "What did you have in mind?"

She ignored her aunt's startled, "Carina!"

"Well if you intended to drive a phaeton, three
is rather a crowd. Perhaps you might prefer to
drive Elizabeth alone and take me riding some
other time?" She raised limpid eyes to his face
and, emboldened by the clear amusement depict-
ed there, rushed on despite her aunt's anguished

glance. "The only problem is that I do not as yet have a horse here in London."

Gazing thoughtfully at the hopeful little face upturned to his, Gavin was aware of a wave of pity directed toward those whose occupation it would be to prevent this impulsive scamp from ruining herself before she had learned how to go on—if indeed she ever did.

"I would be delighted to have your company on a ride through the park two days from now," he assured her promptly, "and of course I insist on providing a suitable mount." He enjoyed the first look of warm approval that had yet been directed toward him from those disastrously candid eyes and added quizzically, "Nothing too placid, I assume?"

This time he was rewarded with a dazzling smile that revealed dimples in both cheeks. "I prefer a horse with spirit," she returned demurely.

He laughed indulgently and, warmed by a grateful look from Elizabeth, was on the point of departing when the butler appeared in the doorway and announced:

"Sir Edward Lynton, madam."

Miss Silverdown looked at the tall figure coming into view behind Coleman. "Why, Edward, what a pleasant surprise! It's good to see you, my dear boy. I declare you have been positively avoiding us these past two years."

As Sir Edward approached to bow over Miss Silverdown's extended hand, Gavin noted his quick glance at Elizabeth whose face retained all of its customary serenity though she seemed curiously still, and then a warm look directed to Carina who seized his hands joyously.

"Oh, Edward, it's been simply ages! How I've missed you. Is this not a marvelous surprise, Liza?"

Elizabeth smiled and extended her hand which was enfolded in Sir Edward's large one for a moment. "Indeed it is," she agreed cordially. "We do not see nearly enough of you, Edward. Oh," turning toward Gavin, "may I make you gentlemen known to each other?"

"Unnecessary, my dear Elizabeth," replied Sir Edward in his slow fashion. "Gavin and I are old friends. It was he who informed me of your presence in town. I was unaware that you had returned." The two men shook hands cordially.

Elizabeth colored faintly at the slight hint of rebuke, but before she could reply he had turned again to Carina to survey her through his quizzing glass. She stood demurely but mischief danced in her eyes during his lazy scrutiny.

"Now you must say, 'Lord how you've grown, Carina,'" she prompted impishly.

"You've grown up, Carina," he replied quietly, giving her his rare warm smile.

"I'm to have a dance next week. We did not know you were in town either, but you will come, won't you?"

"Of course, if your aunt invites me." The look that accompanied this remark was directed more toward Elizabeth than Miss Silverdown, and both ladies were quick to echo Carina's invitation.

"Now please do sit down all of you," begged Miss Silverdown. "I am developing a permanent ache in my neck from looking up."

Gavin refused since he had been about to leave when Sir Edward's arrival had intervened. After

Coleman had ushered him out, the others settled down to exchange news from the country as Sir Edward's estate was located a short four miles from Ravenshill.

Then Miss Silverdown brought the conversation back to their departed visitor. "I am delighted to find you acquainted with Mr. Delawney, Edward, for we knew nothing at all about him, although we are extremely grateful to him, of course, for his timely assistance yesterday," she added hastily after intercepting a hotly indignant glance from Carina and one of gentle rebuke from Elizabeth. "I gather he acquainted you with the facts of that unfortunate situation?"

"Yes, you were most fortunate that he appeared at the right moment, although he gave most of the credit to Carina's quick action," he replied, smiling at Carina's sudden blush. "Gavin Delawney could be described as an extremely eligible *parti*," he continued quietly, seemingly unaware of Elizabeth's heightened color. "He is already in full possession of a handsome fortune and resides when in London in a large house in Cavendish Square. As to his habits, he is not one of the Peep-o'-Day Boys but is extremely partial to all sports, is a member of the Four Horse Club, and, I believe, a popular favorite among the town's hostesses."

"It could scarcely be otherwise," replied Miss Silverdown rather tartly, "with those credentials. Would I err in assuming he is especially sought after by those hostesses who possess daughters of marriageable age?"

"No, you would not err, ma'am."

"Well, then," Carina said briskly, "I need not

fear to have embarrassed him when I told him I should need a horse to go riding if he is so rich."

"As to that, young woman," said her aunt severely, recalled from her pleasant musings with regard to Mr. Gavin Delawney, "you have behaved in a shockingly crude fashion and it must not be allowed to happen again. Mr. Delawney may have seemed merely amused, but I am persuaded that was due to his fine sensibility and forbearance with your extreme youth. No doubt he has marked you down as a mannerless hoyden. I can only be thankful no third party was present to witness such forwardness."

"Please, Aunt," Elizabeth broke in gently, noticing her sister's crestfallen expression and the mild amusement and sympathy in Edward's faintly smiling eyes. "Carina is very young and I think was betrayed into unseemly conduct by Mr. Delawney's easy manner toward her, almost as if she were a young sister. I think she will behave with more formality to the young men she will meet in the course of her presentation."

Carina smiled gratefully at her sister. "I promise to be a pattern card of propriety with all these other nameless young men."

"But not with Mr. Delawney?" Edward interpolated teasingly.

"Well, no, he does not seem like the formal type. Besides, he deliberately tries to provoke me," she added not quite truthfully.

Miss Silverdown and Elizabeth both protested that Mr. Delawney's manner toward Carina could not be faulted, but she had the last word.

"Well, if he is besotted with Liza he will simply have to put up with me, won't he?"

Both ladies hastened to divert the conversation then and succeeded in avoiding any further mention of Mr. Gavin Delawney during the remainder of Edward's brief visit.

CHAPTER 3

The pace of life in the house on Green Street quickened agreeably during the days remaining before Carina's ball. Several of Miss Silverdown's old friends called to welcome her to London and make the acquaintance of her nieces. Elizabeth had met some of them during her curtailed season and was happy to see Carina, before her own dance, introduced to many who would be her hostesses. Among their callers during the next week were no less than three of the six patronesses of Almack's, that hallowed club known to the irreverent as the Marriage Mart. One might forgo a court presentation and still be said to inhabit the upper strata of Society, but if denied admission to Almack's, one's social banishment was complete and irrevocable.

Miss Silverdown's strictures to hold her tongue and not push herself forward in any way, coupled with Elizabeth's gentle hints not to give way to unseemly levity when in the company of any of these dragons, had temporarily cowed Carina into a state of insipid propriety, at least insofar as one of her zestful spirit could conform to social formulas. In the somewhat daunting presence of Mrs. Drummond-Burrell and Countess Lieven she confined herself to small polite smiles and spoke only when directly addressed. Her lovely voice was a decided asset, but in the absence of her usual vivacity her looks paled to insignificance beside the classically beautiful Elizabeth. In combination with this, her tininess operated on the minds of the disinterested in a way that made it almost inevitable that they should dismiss her as likely to cause scant rippling on the social sea. Elizabeth Raven was another matter entirely. Not only was she a diamond of the first water and a well-bred and well-behaved young woman, but her fortune assured her of a high place among the more eligible debutantes of the season. Carina's status in this respect was shrewdly assessed as negligible, for Matthew Raven's weakness for gambling was no secret amongst the more knowing members of the ton. As his estate had never been more than moderate before his wife died, Carina's eligibility was thus quite correctly evaluated.

After her encounter with the more formidable of the patronesses, it was with a sense of delighted relief that she made the discovery that Lady Jersey was an entirely different kettle of fish. Known to her intimates and enemies as Silence, her continuous inconsequential chatter concealed a shrewd understanding. She could be a regrettably high stickler and had been known to administer crushing setdowns to those guilty of encroaching manners, but she was of a capricious nature, and those persons she took a fancy to were assured of solid social backing.

She arrived most inopportunely one morning just as Carina, who was a born mimic, was animatedly characterizing a social-climbing acquaintance for Elizabeth's mild amusement and the wholehearted, slightly malicious enjoyment of Miss Silverdown who had experienced on more than one occasion the too-gracious condescension of the lady in question. The usually impeccable Coleman, in a moment of what he later described almost tearfully to Miss Silverdown as mental aberration, stopped thunderstruck on the threshold, thus permitting Lady Jersey, who was almost at his side, a ringside seat, as it were, for this uninhibited performance. He recovered almost immediately, but not, as he bitterly remarked when relating the unfortunate incident to Mrs. Coleman, before Lady Jersey had received the full impression of Miss Carina in one of her starts. He cleared his throat and announced in more sonorous tones than usual:

"Lady Jersey!"

None of the occupants of the drawing room had heard the door open so engrossed as they were in Carina's antics. Miss Silverdown and Elizabeth looked up startled and Carina, blushing furiously, was unable to move a muscle for an instant.

Lady Jersey entered in a rustle of skirts and on a tinkling laugh.

"No, pray do not stop on my account—Lady Meecham to the last nuance—'my cousin, the duke,' indeed." She paused and surveyed Carina thoroughly. "You are very clever, my dear, but you must take care where you display this particular talent." Her laughter trilled again. "One is almost tempted to . . . no, that would not do of course, but I can see that the Assembly Rooms will be a bit livelier this season."

She turned to greet Miss Silverdown and Elizabeth, giving Carina a welcome opportunity to compose herself. Presently she offered a shy apology that was brushed aside by Lady Jersey.

"Never apologize for unconventional behavior, my child, if you wish to carry it off successfully."

Having heard Mrs. Burrell's opinion of Carina Raven, she was rather surprised to behold not a colorless little dab of a girl but this sparkling creature with the most magnificent gray eyes imaginable. There was no denying her lack of inches constituted a drawback and she was definitely not in the established mode, but insignificant with those fantastic eyes and flower petal skin? Never that. She was not at all sure she approved of the red hair but her figure was faultless. Also it was obvious that she possessed more liveliness than her sister. Elizabeth Raven, she mused while smoothly carrying on more than her share of the conversation, was a beautiful girl and very modestly behaved for one who had been a sensation for a brief time last year and would undoubtedly be just as sought after this season. She accorded her intelligence and a well-bred ease of manner, but there was perhaps a want of spirit which made her a trifle insipid. It was a safe guess that the little one did not lack this quality; in fact, she probably possessed far too much spirit. Yes indeed, this season should prove most interesting with the addition of the Raven sisters to the ranks of the debutantes. If her fortune had been at all respectable, which it could not be with Matthew Raven for a father, she would have felt assured in predicting that Carina would become the rage. Even without the advantages of fortune she might

do very well indeed. By the time she had made
her adieux, Lady Jersey had begun casting about
in her mind for suitable gentlemen to present to
Carina who did not labor under the necessity of
seeking a rich wife.

The visitors to the Raven household were not
all influential dowagers during this interval however. Of Mr. Gavin Delawney they had seen
much. On several occasions he called to see how
the ladies did or to take Elizabeth and Carina
driving or riding.

He had enjoyed his first drive with Elizabeth
enormously, finding her intelligent and convers-
able as well as beautiful. Nor did she display any
of the affectations to be expected in one so lovely.
He was well aware that she would be increasingly
sought after once the word got around that she
was back in town, and he was determined to press
his advantage early. In this admirable tactical
plan he had not allowed for the almost constant
presence of her uninhibited young sister, however.
Not that he disliked Carina. On the contrary,
from the moment of presenting himself for their
ride with a beautiful, spirited little chestnut mare
for her use, she had ceased sparring with him and
to his mild surprise proved to be amicable and
quite companionable. Indeed she treated him like
the brother she had once expressed a wish to
have. He had grown up with a younger sister,
now married, and found himself sliding into the
same easy relationship with Carina he had enjoyed with Isabella during his youth.

No, certainly he did not begrudge the time
spent riding with Carina, but he would have been
pleased to discover that Elizabeth wished to ride

or drive out with him alone. However the most careful observation could discern no such wish on her part. It was true that well-brought-up young ladies would scorn to cast out lures, but Mr. Delawney had had enough success with the fair sex to recognize partiality even in a very correct young lady. To his chagrin Elizabeth displayed no such partiality. Mr. Delawney was not easily cast into despair, however, nor was he one to languish after even the fairest damsel.

This was brought forcibly home to the sisters when they glimpsed him during one of their frequent shopping expeditions to Bond Street. Not that Mr. Delawney was shopping as Carina later related to Miss Silverdown. He was driving a rather pretty brunette in his phaeton and was being so well entertained that he did not even see the Raven sisters. At least Miss Silverdown gathered from Elizabeth's casual comment that the female passenger was attractive. Carina, who was inclined to be resentful on her sister's behalf, would not allow that the young woman in question was even passably good-looking.

Miss Silverdown glanced at her younger niece appraisingly.

"Is there any reason why Mr. Delawney should not drive this young woman or a hundred young women in his phaeton?"

Carina noted the faint amusement in Elizabeth's eyes and sputtered indignantly, "Well, but he was bowled out by Liza the instant he clapped eyes on her and you cannot deny he has been trying to fix his interest with her ever since."

"Nonsense," Miss Silverdown answered forthrightly. "He has been flatteringly attentive, of course, but it is far too soon to say he is trying to fix his interest with Elizabeth."

"But if that is so, then he is no better than a ... a flirt!" declared Carina roundly.

Both her aunt and Elizabeth burst out laughing at her outraged expression.

"You have a lot to learn," said Miss Silverdown with unusual dryness as she left the saloon to search for the housekeeper.

Elizabeth was more gentle. "But you know, Dearest, I think he is."

"Is what?"

"A flirt. We never chanced to meet last year when I made my come-out, but I believe I recall several of the girls with whom I became friendly discussing him once and they said he was very popular but their mamas had warned them not to form a *tendre* for him because he was held to be rather fickle and not really interested in settling down."

"Is that why you have not given him any encouragement?"

Elizabeth hesitated for an instant then replied only, "Partly."

If she hoped to discourage Carina from further probing, she was mistaken in her estimate of her sister's tenacity.

"What other reasons have you?" she inquired interestedly.

Again Elizabeth hesitated. "None really, except that I do *not* feel a *tendre* for him. I like him very well but that is all there is to say to it."

Carina was rather disappointed. "He is most amusing company. I think I would like to have him for a brother-in-law. Perhaps you will develop a *tendre* for him when you get to know him better," she suggested hopefully.

"Perhaps," said Elizabeth and turned the subject.

Of their oldest friend, Sir Edward Lynton, the girls saw practically nothing. It is true that he came to take them riding one afternoon, but Carina at least found the outing strangely flat. She was greatly attached to their neighbor and had many happy memories of time spent riding with Elizabeth and Edward in the country though they had seen little of him for the last year or two. He had always been very kind to both girls, and so he was now, but somehow a degree of formality had crept into his manner toward them which disturbed Carina. Elizabeth seemed to notice nothing amiss but treated him with a shade of reserve that faintly puzzled her more outgoing sister. She supposed they must expect changes in old relationships as they grew older, but *she* felt just the same toward Edward as she always had and was vaguely troubled by his attitude. When she mentioned it to Elizabeth afterward, her sister shrugged and passed it off lightly, which unusual callousness only added to Carina's sense of unease.

It was therefore with relief mixed with pleasure that she came into the yellow saloon the following afternoon to find Gavin Delawney seated with her sister and aunt. Flirtatiousness must, of course, be reckoned a serious defect of character, but although she could no longer precisely admire him, there was no reason not to continue to enjoy his company—and his horse, she added a trifle guiltily. She pushed aside the errant thought that her own character might not stand up to a close examination and greeted the smiling young man with her usual friendliness.

The two had soon got upon first-name terms, and though Miss Silverdown's eyebrows rose, she forbore to make any stronger protest as their caller saluted her niece with deplorable informality:

"Hallo, Carina, are you in the mood for a canter in the park?" When was she not? he added mentally, enjoying the way her small face grew animated and her eyes sparkled with anticipation.

"I would love it," she answered promptly, "if my aunt permits." She cast an appealing look at Miss Silverdown who sighed inaudibly but acquiesced somewhat reluctantly. This young man was a shade too particular in his attentions but it must be admitted the atmosphere of the house deteriorated when Carina had been cooped up for any length of time. Her vitality and bursting spirits needed outlets and there was no question of Mr. Delawney going beyond the line of proper conduct with a very young girl. He treated Carina like a young sister and it was really quite thoughtful of him to devote so much time to her. Then he spoke again and she realized too late his real motive.

"I have brought another horse with me in the hope that Miss Raven will also join us. Do you care for a ride today?"

His smile could coax the birds out of the trees, Miss Silverdown was willing to admit but not, seemingly, Elizabeth onto a horse.

"Thank you, another time if I may. I have been feeling a trifle out of sorts today and prefer to remain quiet."

Carina added her entreaties, but when Elizabeth remained firm, she hastened to her room to change into her habit.

Elizabeth's smile could not be faulted either thought her aunt indulgently. A pity she did not seem to favor this lad above others. They made a handsome couple and he was certainly too eligible to be thought a fortune hunter. She would have dozens of that ilk trailing in her wake soon enough. And too gentle to repulse them thoroughly either. Unless he wished to see his elder daughter and her healthy fortune leg-shackled to a smooth-tongued fortune hunter, Matthew Raven had best bestir himself and cast the mantle of his protection over his children for once.

Carina was back in a very few minutes, slightly breathless from hurrying. Gavin laughed at her as he took his leave of the other ladies.

"You certainly do not possess that generally accepted feminine trait of dawdling over your dressing."

Carina looked surprised. "Oh, but you would not wish to keep the horses waiting long, surely?"

Gavin smiled again but made no answer. His groom was outside with the three horses. Carina greeted him with a friendly smile.

"Miss Raven will not be riding today, Finkston. You may return Rufus to the stables and meet us in the park."

"Very good, sir." He smiled at Carina, whose riding had won his admiration, and rode off leading Rufus.

Carina was talking gently to Firefly who nuzzled her shoulder.

"Does your sister not care for riding?" Gavin inquired as he assisted Carina to mount. She allowed the little chestnut a few dancing paces before reining her in, then watched admiringly as he swung effortlessly astride the large black he had been riding the evening he rescued them on Hounslow. As they started off together she answered his question:

"We rode yesterday with Edward so Liza may be a bit stiff today. She used to enjoy riding in the country but has not done much of it here in London. She was never quite so fond of it as I am, however."

"You are a very accomplished horsewoman," he conceded, but made her a teasing bow that robbed the words of any attempt at gallantry. He'd offered her gallantry before, he recalled with amusement.

This time she took him seriously. "I know I am," she answered calmly. "I have spent simply years on a horse so it would be surprising, indeed shameful if I were not accomplished by this time."

He slowed his black to a walk and looked at her with mock severity. "What is shameful, Miss Raven, is your way of receiving compliments. Do you not yet know that a lady blushes and disclaims?"

Carina grinned. "Try me again. I shall do better now that I have had the benefit of your vast experience with women!"

"Allow me to tell you that you are an accomplished horsewoman, Miss Raven," he repeated obligingly.

Carina fluttered her fantastic eyelashes and ducked her head bashfully. "La, sir," she simpered with a slight lisp, "you are too kind. I am but the merest novice, I assure you. If it were not for this marvelous horse of yours, I declare I should probably be unseated by now."

Gavin glared at her. "You are a brass-faced little gypsy and stop that giggling. It is not an accomplishment that I admire. Shall we try again? Do you have any other accomplishments, Miss Raven?"

"Only one, I sing."

"No, no, no! A lady never *claims* a talent. You must say, 'I sing a little, but I fear my voice is not above the ordinary'."

"Why should I say such a thing if it is not true? My teacher, Maestro Bertoldi, says my voice is extraordinary."

Gavin looked disapprovingly at the animated little face, read the mischief in the cool gray eyes and held up a hand in a fencer's gesture of defeat. "I give up; it is of no use to try to guide you. You are an abominable brat and will not doubt sink yourself below reproach before you have been out a sennight."

"No doubt," she echoed cheerfully and pressed her heels into Firefly's side, for they had entered on the park's paths. It was a gray, threatening day and there were few riders and fewer strollers. They were thus able to enjoy a good canter. Gavin, slightly behind, watched her affectionately. The brat had style on a horse, he acknowledged, and even achieved a sort of dignity such a little one would find hard to command in most situations. As he pulled into position beside her, she turned a radiant face to him, and he was struck again by the neatness of her small figure in a severely tailored black habit. The only color was provided by her glowing, peach-tinged cheeks

and lips and the dark fire of her hair. As usual
when they were riding he felt in perfect charity
with her, so it was with some reluctance that he
now spoke.

"I regret that we shall have to curtail our ride a
bit today, brat, but I have an appointment on
Bond Street in half an hour."

She looked disappointed but reined in obediently, and they turned back, walking the horses
now. Finkston, who had not joined them in the
brisk canter, came up behind them and the small
party proceeded toward Green Street.

"I wish now that I had not agreed to meet Ned
today," he offered apologetically.

"At number thirteen, I presume?"

One dark red brow escalated. "Quite correct,
but what would a child like you know about number thirteen Bond Street?"

"I know that it is Gentleman Jackson's and that
gentlemen go there to hit each other which seems
to me a nonsensical thing to do."

"Naturally, for you are a female," he replied
calmly. "To many men like myself boxing is an
enjoyable form of healthy exercise. It might also
be a useful skill to possess if ever one should be
called upon to defend oneself against an aggressor."

"Well, I cannot see anything particularly
healthy about two men hitting each other until
one of them can no longer get to his feet, at least
for the one who is unable to rise," she pointed out
in a reasonable tone.

"I am afraid you have been misinformed, my
child. That is not what goes on at Jackson's."

"That is certainly what happens at a mill,

though; at least," she amended conscientiously, "that was the way it was at the one I saw."

They had approached the Raven house during this last exchange and Gavin had just extended his arms to assist her to dismount. At this last statement his fingers bit into her waist and he froze, staring up at her calm face in stupefied silence for an instant.

"What did you say? Women do not attend mills. That cock won't fight, my dear."

"I do not tell lies," returned Carina indignantly, "at least not very often. I did attend a mill once. Of course I was dressed as a boy at the time. Please, Gavin, you are hurting me," she finished somewhat breathlessly.

He loosened his grip on her immediately, and even in his preoccupation with her words was fleetingly conscious of how very tiny and graceful she was as he swung her down to the ground. He had been frowning furiously, but with an effort forced his features to an expressionless mask as he indicated to the hovering groom that he take the horses, including his own black. Finkston moved off somewhat reluctantly after Carina had bestowed a valedictory smile on him and a loving pat on the chestnut's white-starred forehead. Only when Finkston had moved out of earshot did Gavin turn back to his unconscious companion and demand in grating accents:

"Just when and where did you attend a mill?"

Carina frowned at his tone, and the expression of restrained disgust on his face caused her to lift her chin in defiance. "It is of course none of your affair—but," she added hastily, seeing his face take on a darker color, "it was last year in Littleton.

The scheduled mill was all the stable boys could talk about for weeks and I became so curious I persuaded Robbie to take me along."

"You went to a mill dressed like a boy in the company of a stable hand?" he demanded incredulously. "Good lord, have you no delicacy of mind, no proper feminine instincts?"

"None at all," she returned in a flat little voice, for his obvious censure hurt her more than she was prepared to admit. "Unless you count the fact that I found the whole affair grossly overrated and more brutal than skillful."

He continued to stare at her as though she were some alien creature while she pulled the bell and thanked him coolly for taking her riding.

"The pleasure was all mine, ma'am." His cold formality extended to the bow he made her as the porter opened the door, and he walked rapidly down the street without looking back.

Carina entered the house with a proudly erect gait and a calm countenance, but her spirits were not of the same high order. If the truth, which she had no intention of confessing, be known, she was feeling rather ashamed of herself. She had been deliberately provocative in her behavior and had only herself to blame that Gavin now had good cause to think her a mannerless hoyden unfit for polite society. Resolutely she concealed her inner turbulence to reply with assumed brightness to her aunt's inquiries regarding her ride.

CHAPTER 4

Monsieur Alexandre was shown into the small saloon where the three ladies awaited him on the morning of Carina's ball. His appearance was a revelation to the younger girl who had not yet encountered a thoroughgoing dandy. Her eye was immediately drawn to a coat of the most virulent shade of green and from there to a flowered waistcoat with several dangling fobs. His skintight pantaloons of bright yellow unfortunately revealed that his legs were inclined to bow out, but any inadequacies in shoulders or chest had been amply disguised by considerable padding. The wasp-waisted jacket bore huge buttons of mother-of-pearl and his enormously wide neckcloth was tied in a complex arrangement that forced his chin to be held at an unnatural angle, giving him an appearance of perpetual inquiry further reinforced by a pair of thick, black, arching eyebrows. His normally sallow complexion reflected a green tinge from his coat and his skin was pulled taut over gaunt cheeks. The slightly cadaverous effect was enhanced by a long, thin nose and a wide, thin-lipped mouth. His long, wildly curling black hair failed to conceal the fact that his large ears stuck out from his head at a rather oblique angle. Of indeterminate age, moderate height and lean build, his person would have been totally unprepossessing if a pair of large and very fine eyes of dark liquid brown had not redeemed his appearance. These eyes were bright, alert and very kind. In conjunction with a gap-toothed smile that infused life into the otherwise unpromising cast of features, they conveyed the inherent gentle nature of the man.

After her initial surprise at his appearance, Carina took an immediate liking to him and was more willing to entrust herself to his hands than were her aunt and sister. He had greeted Elizabeth ecstatically and fervently kissed her hand.

"Ah, the so beautiful Miss Raven with the hair of new gold. You wish Alexandre to create for you a new coiffure for evening, *n'est-ce pas?*"

Elizabeth withdrew her hand gently and explained that it was her sister who wished a new hairstyle.

Alexandre's fine eyes considered Carina thoroughly and he slowly circled her tiny figure, weighing her appearance as if she were a steer at the market, she thought with amusement. She remained still, but her eyes were dancing with mischief when the normally voluble Frenchman had completed his silent survey. Seeing this, his own wide smile erupted and he snapped his fingers in delight.

"Ah, *la petite* is an original. Everything about her is perfection except for the impossible hair. The color is unique *je crois, vraiment?*—but there is too much." Both hands described open gestures on either side of Carina's head, then proceeded to lift her hair away from her face. "*Voyez,* the shape of the head, perfection, the small flat ears, perfection." He tipped up her chin and turned her face away. "The profile like that of the angels in the old paintings, but the so wild hair conceals all this perfection. It must go, all of it," he finished with a dramatic gesture.

Carina giggled at the identical expressions adorning the faces of her sister and aunt which seemed to be compounded of equal parts of anticipation and doubt.

Elizabeth found her voice first. "But, Monsieur Alexandre, no one wears really short hair. It is . . . unfeminine and she would be unable to change styles for the evening. It is too heavy of course; some must be cut but not too short," she protested feebly.

"All of it," Monsieur Alexandre insisted firmly. "You must trust me. I must have your entire confidence if I am to create a work of art of Mlle. Carina. She will set a new style; she will become the rage. I guarantee it, *absolument*." He struck his closed fist over his heart.

Elizabeth still looked doubtful, but Miss Silverdown, head on one side, was staring intently at her younger niece with narrowed eyes. "You know, Elizabeth," she murmured slowly, "Carina does have a look about her of those Greek statues we were looking at recently. She will never be in the accepted mode in any case, so why not let her set her own style?"

"Yes, Liza," begged Carina, "I am so tired of brushing this heavy hair. I think I should prefer it short."

"Well . . ." Elizabeth was still reluctant. "Why not cut some off and see how it becomes you before we decide on an unfashionably short crop?"

Alexandre murmured something that could have been taken for assent, but Carina was persuaded he meant to have his own way in the end. There was a fanatical light in the liquid eyes which were again studying her, but she suffered no such qualms as Liza appeared to feel. Her hair was a bother and she detested the color anyway. What did it signify whether or not she wore it in the current style?

"Cut it please," she said, dimpling at Monsieur Alexandre who beamed a benevolent smile back at her.

Elizabeth subsided, still doubtful but silent now, and Alexandre proceeded to cut Carina's heavy tresses. This was accomplished in total silence, though Carina was hard put to conquer an absurd desire to giggle as her interested gaze roamed from Monsieur Alexandre's intent face to Miss Silverdown's hopeful countenance to Liza, sitting tensely apprehensive as the strands of fiery hair drifted down onto the floor.

Twenty minutes later Carina ended the silence as Monsieur Alexandre swept the towel from her shoulders with a flourish and assisted her to rise from the bench on which she had been sitting. Her smile was a bit uncertain.

"The thirteen-year-old boy again," she said wryly.

Elizabeth released a long breath and relaxed her clasped hands. "Yes, but this time with a difference," she said quietly, her smile not at all uncertain.

"*Vive la différence*," intoned Alexandre pontifically, kissing his fingertips to the younger girl who bobbed him a curtsy before turning to her aunt with a question in her eyes.

Miss Silverdown's faded blue eyes were clouded with emotion. "You look lovely, child. How thrilled your mother would have been to see you today. That short, curly style suits you completely."

Carina hugged her convulsively, then turned to the smiling Frenchman. "Thank you so much, Monsieur Alexandre. This feels so much freer and lighter." She gave her head a little shake, and the sunlight streaming in from the long windows caught the imprisoned little flames as she moved her head. Carina had a perfectly oval face and Monsieur Alexandre had not allowed any hair to blur the lovely outline, but now he leaned forward and flicked a curling strand of hair to a position on her forehead slanting toward one curved brow.

"For the daytime back for symmetry, for the evening one or two curls forward, *comme ça*, to torment your admirers." At Carina's questioning glance he explained, "Every man you meet will yearn to push that stray lock of hair back into place."

She looked faintly alarmed. "Surely no one will touch my hair," she protested.

Her aunt was impatient with this naiveté. "Carina, you are old enough to know that no gentleman would touch your person except to guide or assist you."

Elizabeth smiled tenderly at her. "Of course not, Dearest. Monsieur Alexandre is merely being flattering. You must expect compliments now."

Carina was remembering her sister's words

hours later as Abby pulled forward a lock of hair in the same way as Monsieur Alexandre had done and she frowned at the girl in the mirror. She did not look like herself at all, and while part of her was excited by the new image staring back at her, the rest of her brain was a bit uneasy. She absolutely loved to dance, but if her partners were to pay her ridiculous compliments, all her pleasure in the evening would be destroyed. As Elizabeth entered her bedchamber to supervise the final touches to her sister's toilette, Carina turned to her in a near panic.

"Liza, what shall I do if gentlemen pay me foolish compliments? But perhaps they will not after all," she reassured herself. "Surely Monsieur Alexandre is a rather extravagant person? Other men won't talk the way he does, will they?"

Elizabeth laughed merrily. "You look ravishing, Dearest, and must be prepared for all manner of compliments. Try not to let them embarrass you."

"But how do I reply?"

"Just smile and say thank you and turn the subject to some commonplace. Refrain from calling anyone a liar," she added mischievously, "even if you believe their praises are not wholly sincere."

"Liza, even I know better than to do such a thing," returned Carina indignantly, but she dimpled and her moment of stage fright was over.

If her father's reaction to her appearance was typical, she need not have worried about how to reply to compliments, she thought wryly a few minutes later in the great saloon.

"Well," he drawled, after subjecting her to a close scrutiny, "there is no look of your mother about you, but you are better than I thought."

"You overwhelm me, Papa," she replied demurely.

"Little minx," he grinned tolerantly. "I imagine you'll turn a few heads at that." He looked at his elder daughter in complete silence, and they knew by the pain in his eyes that he was thinking of their mother.

Elizabeth was stunningly beautiful in rose pink silk, her lovely bare shoulders gleaming and smooth in the light of hundreds of candles. The brilliance turned her hair to silver-gilt and deepened the blue of her eyes while the fragile diamond pendant about her throat sparkled and flashed. The necklace had belonged to their mother. Elizabeth had insisted that Carina wear her pearls since the only jewelry the younger girl had inherited was a rather old-fashioned set of garnets that had belonged to her paternal grandmother and a gold filigree necklace that while lovely was a bit too old for her as yet.

The two girls combined their efforts to divert their father's thoughts by touring him around the flower-bedecked room and telling him about some of the guests who were expected. They had written him of the attempted holdup, of course, and now reminded him that Mr. Delawney would be among their guests so that Mr. Raven could tender his paternal thanks for the rescue.

"And Edward promised to look in also, Papa," said Carina gaily. "We did not even know he was in town, but it seems he and Gavin are well acquainted and he came to see us after Gavin had told him about our adventure."

"Has Lynton been haunting the place?" Mr.

Raven asked rather sharply, directing the question not at Carina but Elizabeth.

"Indeed no, Papa," she returned quietly. "We have seen very little of Edward."

He continued to stare at her for a few seconds but her face remained serene.

Several hours later the serenely beautiful face of Miss Elizabeth Raven was the first sight to impress itself on Mr. Gavin Delawney as he entered one of the large saloons which, in the absence of a ballroom, had been thrown open to accommodate about seventy couples for dancing. He made his way through a crowd of persons that seemed to number double this, bowing and smiling to acquaintances but not permitting himself to be waylaid by old friends or young women with inviting smiles, to attain a place at her side. Catching sight of his red hair as he wove his determined way through the press of people, she smiled and laid a detaining hand on the arm of the middle-aged man beside her.

"Your very obedient servant, Miss Raven," Gavin said, smiling into her eyes.

"I am so happy you were able to come, Mr. Delawney. "Father, may I present Mr. Gavin Delawney to whom we are vastly indebted?"

"How do you do, sir?" he said politely, having already recognized the slim man with the graying red hair from his likeness to Carina. "I fear Miss Raven exaggerates the small service I was able to render."

"Not at all, my boy. I too wish to extend my heartfelt gratitude for your timely intervention last week. My sister-in-law and my daughters have told me the whole story. You are too modest. Please accept my sincere thanks."

Slightly embarrassed, Gavin was pleased to make greeting Miss Silverdown, who had approached them during this speech, an excuse to change the subject. She too was looking most elegant in a deep purple gown with fine Brussels lace. After exchanging a few desultory remarks with Mr. Raven, he reminded Elizabeth that she had promised him a dance just in time to forstall two gentlemen who were rapidly closing in from different directions as the music started up again.

She acquiesced laughingly and he swept her onto the floor under the approving eye of Miss Silverdown who thought them quite the handsomest couple in the room, and the furious glances of the gentlemen who had been thwarted and who seemed to find the sight of them much less pleasing. Her dancing, like everything else about her, was perfection, and his spirits climbed as the delightful interval lengthened. For truth to tell, Gavin had not been entirely complacent about coming this evening. He knew the most he could expect was one dance with Elizabeth and he had parted from Carina with much annoyance at their last meeting. At first he had been inclined to censure her severely for her unseemly behavior, but Carina was very likable, and as his temper cooled he revoked his first hasty decision to have nothing further to do with her. He did wonder how she would take, though, and found himself rather anxious on her behalf. She was entirely capable of committing some outrageous blunder that would earn her snubs from the more straitlaced of the town's hostesses, and he did not wish this to happen for her sister's sake as well as her own. He had stayed away from the Raven household for the past two days but in the end had relented and sent her a nosegay for the dance. He had sent Elizabeth flowers too and was pleased to see she was carrying the bouquet for which she thanked him charmingly.

As the dance drew to a close, he still had not sighted Carina, and then suddenly a group of people moved past, revealing the young girl surrounded by several gentlemen, all of whom seemed entranced with her. He drew a quick breath and studied her covertly while leading Elizabeth toward the group. His first reaction was a very natural admiration at the adorable picture she presented in her filmy white gown and his second, hard on the heels of the first, was an unusual prick of irritation on discovering that the nosegay she carried was not his token. Knowing she had a partiality for yellow he had specified yellow ribbons, and the bouquet she carried was all white. She turned to answer a remark from one of her escorts, and he was struck for the first time by the exquisite proportions of the proudly carried little head on her long slender neck. With the long heavy hair cropped to this halo of curls, the delicacy of her bone structure and the purity of her profile were revealed as outstandingly lovely. His gaze fell to the expanse of smooth creamy skin left bare by a fairly low-cut bodice. Her figure was flawless too—in fact, the child was breathtakingly lovely, a veritable Pocket Venus.

The uneasy feeling of strangeness, that here was a Carina he did not know, vanished as she glanced up and grinned impishly when she saw him approaching with her sister. "Gavin, at last. I feared you meant to punish me by not coming to my ball."

The half-enchanted spell cast by her loveliness was immediately replaced by a familiar feeling of exasperation. Good lord, did the brat mean to reveal to the world what had passed between them at their last meeting?

"You wound me, Miss Carina," he inserted smoothly, deriving a malicious satisfaction in her surprise at this method of address, "with your unfounded accusations. I am here to claim the dance you promised me. If you will excuse us, gentlemen," he added, after making sure Elizabeth's next partner had claimed her.

He was smiling attentively as he led her into the dance, but his pose of eager swain fell from him abruptly when he was sure no one could overhear. His voice dripped icicles:

"Would I be doing you an injustice, little one, if I assumed you were on the brink of detailing our last unfortunate conversation to all and sundry?"

"Indeed you would," she answered smartly. "Of course I had no intention of telling anyone else."

"Well, that is a weight off my mind. I had quite decided your disastrous frankness extended to all your acquaintance."

Carina looked hurt. Gavin seemed quite determined to be uncivil. He had not even asked her if she were enjoying her party. "No, only to you, but I won't do it anymore. I did not mean to give you a disgust of me."

Gavin experienced a quick stab of compunction at her unexpected meekness. She was only a child after all. He squeezed her hand comfortingly and hastily retracted: "No, no, I did not mean that you should feel constraint with me—never that, but only wished to urge you to be circumspect with others."

She brightened at that. "Oh, I am, really. I talk freely to you because you are such a good friend." She smiled confidingly up at him and he realized suddenly that when he had experienced sympathy for those whose reponsibility it was to see she did not ruin herself, he should have included himself amongst them. He had an awful premonition that it would be his unenviable task to keep an eye on her on numerous occasions yet to come. Meanwhile he had a bone to pick with her.

"How is it then that you could not bring yourself to carry the flowers sent to you by such a good friend?"

She said contritely, "I have not even thanked you for them and they are so pretty. I had to carry Edward's, you see, because they are all white and it is usual to present a very virginal appearance at one's ..." She broke off as he choked suddenly. "Are you all right, Gavin?"

"Quite, but, Carina, I beg you not to use that word in your conversations with men," he said in desperate earnest.

"But I only meant to explain ..."

"Thank you, I know the meaning of the word. Carina, I could shake you. You must learn to guard your tongue." He stopped abruptly and summoned up a smile. "Come, let us finish the dance without conversation."

Carina relaxed compliantly and allowed the lilting music to invade her senses. Gavin was a superb dancer and soon they were moving together as if they had practiced for hours. No further conversation was exchanged for some little time. Carina's irrepressible spirits were completely restored by the pleasure of the dance. Later when she glanced up and caught his gaze on the lock of hair on her forehead, she asked brightly:

"Do you yearn to push that hair back?"

Gavin nearly stumbled but recovered just in time to avoid crashing into another couple. "I beg your pardon?"

Seemingly unaware of his frigid accents she enunciated more clearly. "Do you yearn to push my hair back?"

"Certainly not. Where did you get such an idea?"

"Monsieur Alexandre said every man I met would yearn to do so, but I was sure it was all a hum. And so it was," she finished calmly.

He ground his teeth audibly. "And who is Monsieur Alexandre?"

"Goodness, I thought everyone knew him. He is the man who cut my hair."

He relaxed slightly. "I see. Carina please promise me you will not ask anyone else if he yearns to push your hair back."

Her lovely laugh gurgled. "Of course I will not, foolish. I only asked you because you are such a . . ."

"I know, such a good friend. Why you have honored me with your friendship is a question I shall ponder deeply." The music was drawing to a close, and as he led her to where a tall lanky youth was waiting impatiently for the next dance, he bowed and said, "Thank you for the most

eventful dance I can ever recall. It will long linger
in my memory."

Twin devils danced in the smoky eyes but the
lilting voice said sweetly, "It was my pleasure,
sir."

He shot her a suspicious glance but she had already moved away with her impatient partner.
Gavin proceeded slowly toward the supper room
to recruit his flagging spirits with Matthew
Raven's best champagne. He felt he had earned
it. Also he was uneasily aware that he had absolutely no idea whether the previous scene had
been played in innocence or in a spirit of pure
deviltry. That wretched imp was *capable de tout.*
Frowning thoughtfully, he walked past one of his
oldest friends and had to be jerked by the arm
before recognizing him.

As for his recent antagonist she was enjoying
herself hugely. In all her admittedly few years she
had never been so excited nor found anything so
vastly diverting, at least not any activity that was
performed indoors. For the first time ever she had
as much opportunity to dance as she could wish.
She had met any number of young men who did
her the honor to seek her company, and although
she privately considered their fulsome compliments just so much nonsense, she found her sister's advice eminently sound and was able to
parry most personal remarks.

Proceeding into the saloon where supper was
laid, she was smiling secretly to herself, recalling
the rather appalling degree of thoroughness with
which she had determinedly discussed the music
and decorations when her partners seemed to
have no small talk other than pointed gallantry. It

had been with some relief that she accepted Edward's offer to provide her with supper. Her feet in their ridiculously tiny white slippers felt fine but her jaws were beginning to ache from so much bright civility and she was aware of great hallowness within. When Edward asked her preference as to food she declared simply:

"Some of everything, if you please; I am famished."

He laughed and proceeded to fulfill his commission with meticulous care. Returning in a very few moments with a laden tray he accepted her heartfelt thanks solemnly.

"If you succeed in ingesting that lot, I shall have to revise my opinion of your adult status. Only a lumberjack or a growing boy could need that much sustenance."

"And me. I have been dancing for hours and I am empty to my toes." She attacked her plate with healthy relish and demonstrated forthwith the truth of her claim. Conversation was desultory, for Carina was concentrating on delicious lobster patties and pâté, and Edward, who had known her forever, did not feel it incumbent upon himself to entertain her. He had never been much given to small talk, in any case, and the almost silent meal was perfectly comfortable for both. Not that Edward seemed to share the same hollowness as Carina following his exertions on the dance floor. She looked up from a peach ice she was demolishing with pleasure to note Edward's sober glance directed across the room to a table where Elizabeth and another young lady as yet unknown to Carina were being well entertained by Gavin and a curly-headed youth with whom Carina recalled having danced the boulanger.

"Doesn't Liza look beautiful in that deep pink?" she queried conversationally. "How fortunate the ribbons on the nosegay Gavin sent exactly matched it."

"Yes, fortunate," he answered. He had wondered whose gift she had distinguished, having noticed immediately that she was not carrying his flowers. There was a brief silence, then he continued quietly, "Elizabeth looks beautiful in anything."

"Yes, doesn't she? It is not for me to say, of course, but she is easily the loveliest girl here."

He pushed away his practically untouched plate and resolutely returned his gaze from Elizabeth's shining beauty to study his companion fondly.

"There is nothing amiss with the picture you present, my dear. You have grown very lovely."

Carina dimpled at him mischievously. "Did I sound as though I were fishing for compliments, Edward? I assure you it was not the case. I find compliments a dead bore. I would rather dance," she hinted delicately, casting him a provocative glance from under those black lashes.

He smiled affectionately at her and took her hand indulgently to lead her back to the floor. Gavin, who had chanced to glance in their direction, noticed this bit of byplay and thought with faint irritation that the brat was learning fast. Already she was playing games with those potent eyes of hers, and from the fatuous look on Ned's face she had not cast her net in vain. Ridiculous chit, Lynton was much too old for her. Seeing that Elizabeth's serious gaze had followed his, he remarked lightly:

"Your young sister is learning the art of flirtation in record time."

"Carina has known Edward all her life. She is deeply attached to him."

There was no reproof evident in the quiet voice but Gavin knew the subject had been decidedly closed. He considered the lovely girl with him, no, not with him really. Why did he always have the impression in Elizabeth Raven's presence that he was facing a closed door, not a willfully slammed door—she was perfectly charming company—but he knew he had not penetrated some deep reserve that prevented her from being in complete contact with him. Was she like this with everyone or only with him? Then he shook himself mentally as an idiot. After all he had met the girl less than a fortnight before. Carina too, he mused, but Carina's nature was so much more open. He might have been acquainted with her in her cradle the way she treated him.

The sound of music served to wrench him back from his unprofitable musings and he decided to press his luck by claiming another dance with Elizabeth.

CHAPTER 5

During the days immediately following Carina's dance, the slim house on Green Street suffered an influx of callers that gratified the various inhabitants in differing degrees. At one end of the scale stood Abby whose simple pride in her mistresses' popularity shone out of her comely face. She took care however not to display this in the presence of Coleman whose legs seemed to have developed a permanent ache from constantly showing callers up and down stairs, and who ruefully confessed to his better half to having suffered on more than one occasion from a traitorous urge to remove the knocker from the door with his own hand just for a bit of rest.

Somewhere between these two extremes dwelt the ladies of the household, alone again, for Matthew Raven, his paternal duty graciously performed, had removed himself to a less socially demanding vicinity the day after the party. Miss Silverdown viewed their increased social activity with complacency untinged by surprise. After all, Elizabeth had achieved a great success the previous year and nothing had really changed. Naturally Carina would be included in the vast majority of invitations Elizabeth received. This was not to say that Miss Silverdown anticipated it would be possible to achieve a brilliant match for her essentially dowerless younger niece, but since the child was too young to be looking for a husband in any case, she might as well simply concentrate on enjoying her season.

In fact Carina showed every evidence of profiting by this excellent advice. Her head untroubled by any thoughts of marriage, she proceeded to enjoy each day's pleasures as they occurred. If Elizabeth's suitors were in deadly earnest, hoping to fix their interest with this most eligible lady, Carina drew the attention of some of the town's livelier young blades intent upon having the most enjoyable time possible. She was gay and friendly, relaxed and refreshingly matter-of-fact, unlike the majority of her contemporaries who were constantly aware that their main concern was finding a husband to establish them. The only cloud on Carina's horizon, and that a small one, was that their numerous social commitments left less time for riding.

The main source of Elizabeth's quiet satisfaction in their current popularity was the ingenuous delight displayed by her sister in the whirl of new activities opening up to them. She herself was looking forward to introducing Carina to the opera and knew her sister would share her pleasure in theater going. Her own status as one of the most-sought-after girls in society seemed to offer her little real satisfaction. There were a few among her multitude of admirers toward whom she felt a disinterested friendliness, but that none of them stirred her to warmer feelings was only too evident to her sister and aunt. Since she was essentially a kindhearted girl, it gave her no pleasure to refuse those offers she could not prevent, so in the main she tried by her air of cool reserve to discourage her suitors from actually coming to the point. That this policy could not be entirely successful was inevitable, and within two weeks of Carina's dance she had to urge her aunt to deny permission to two persistent suitors to call upon her father. Both of these gentlemen were extremely eligible, and it was with real regret that Miss Silverdown made her niece's feelings known to them.

Carina, who had already selected Gavin Delawney as her choice for a brother-in-law, was relieved but uneasy too. Clearly Elizabeth appreciated his easy company and sparkling wit but no amount of wishful thinking on the part of Miss Silverdown and her sister was sufficient to impute to Elizabeth any deeper regard than friendship. Since no one else at the moment seemed likely to inspire her toward warmer feelings either, Carina was easily able to postpone worrying over the matter in favor of enjoying herself in each new situation.

One of the highlights of any young girl's first season must be her initial visit to Almack's. Lady Jersey had graciously sent them vouchers and Carina eagerly prepared for her debut. Elizabeth had warned her that the rooms while large and bright were not particularly imposing, so she was not disappointed in the decor and did not expect lavish refreshments. She could not be disappointed in the company because it was immediately apparent that, like her sister, Carina Raven was destined to be a success.

She had her pick of attractive partners and could have danced all evening had it not been for that unwritten but inflexible rule prohibiting any lady from participating in the waltz until one of the patronesses had signified her approval. Miss Silverdown had been at great pains to impress this fact of life upon Carina, concealing behind an unusual severity her anxiety lest her impulsive niece might nonchalantly go against this dictum in a spirit of pure mischief if tempted by one of the livelier members of her train. Almack's was considered deadly tame entertainment by many young bloods who might not be averse to enlivening the proceedings by scandalizing the hostesses. However, in this fear she did Carina an injustice, for the girl was conscious of her promise to her sister to behave everywhere with propriety. She laughingly refused to waltz with a young buck whose dancing eyes proclaimed that he had probably been prompted by his friends to solicit her hand in hopes of raising a few eyebrows.

She was joined by her sister who had also excused herself from dancing so that she might keep Carina company, thus lessening the chagrin she might be expected to feel in the face of the pitying glances bestowed upon her by the more favored females as they waltzed past. Since several gentlemen elected to sit and chat with the two Raven sisters in preference to dancing, Carina was spared the humiliation of sitting out the dance amongst the dowagers. They were all conversing amiably when a man approached Elizabeth and claimed her attention.

"It is Miss Raven, is it not? We were introduced briefly last season, ma'am, though amongst so many my name may have escaped you. I am Edgemere, and most delighted to renew our acquaintance."

Elizabeth extended her hand, saying with her cool smile:

"Oh, yes, Lord Edgemere, I do recall being introduced, but not, I think, at Almack's? May I present my sister? Carina, this is Guy Accrington, Earl of Edgemere."

Carina turned her interested gaze upon the handsomest man she had yet encountered in her brief social career. She guessed he was even older than Edward, but he was impressively straight, with a fine pair of shoulders and an athletic build. He was smiling charmingly, displaying perfect teeth in a nicely shaped mouth. Indeed, everything about his appearance was attractive with the possible exception of his eyes. Large and long lashed, they were a shade of amber which contrasted engagingly with his blond locks brushed in a Brutus and his suntanned skin, but Carina experienced a slight jolt to her nervous system on staring into them. The charm of his smile owed nothing whatever to his eyes, she mused, because they were merely watchful and alert with no warmth at all. His classically cut nose and high cheekbones gave his countenance an arresting, clear-cut quality, and she found herself wishing he could turn his head so she might study whether his profile was as handsome as the rest of his features. He did not turn his head immediately, however, for he was being flatteringly attentive to Carina. He had lingered just that fraction of a second too long over her hand and was fer-

vently declaring his pleasure in meeting yet another charming and beautiful Raven sister.

"You are too kind, sir," murmured Carina,
smiling beguilingly up at him while her exotic
eyelashes swept up, revealing amusement deep in
the clear gray eyes.

"Compliments don't move this hardhearted
wench, Edgemere," offered a slight young man
who had quickly become one of Carina's favorite
partners. "You should be advised that she prefers
the word with the bark on it."

"Hush, Tony," commanded Carina, dimpling.
"Lord Edgemere will think me an unnatural female."

The earl acknowledged Sir Anthony Mercer
with a grin and promptly turned his back on him.
Appearing to become aware of the waltz music for
the first time, he smilingly requested the pleasure
of dancing with Miss Carina.

Carina eyed him consideringly. "Well, sir, I
would be delighted, of course, but since I've no
taste for creating talk, I'm afraid I shall have to
decline."

The earl's smile froze for an instant and a wary
look flashed into those amber-lighted eyes.

Tony Mercer hooted with laughter. "No," he
said with falsely sweet solicitude, "it ain't a case
of her already knowing your reputation, Edgemere. The chit is new here; she hasn't been allowed to waltz yet."

Carina was intrigued by this slyly malicious
comment but pretended deafness. She smiled at
the earl, whose features were again composed into
a politely attentive mien, and repeated her
willingness to dance another time.

"I shall remind you of that presently, Miss Carina," he said determinedly and turned to say a few words to Elizabeth, who had been attending to the gentleman on her left, before walking away to join a group of men on the other side of the room.

Carina's eyes followed his progress thoughtfully for a moment then came back to her friend. Tony was not going to get away with dropping sly hints. She would have the truth about the handsome earl before the evening was over. There was no immediate opportunity, however, for the waltz ended and she was claimed by her next partner to make up a set for a country dance.

Just before the doors closed at eleven o'clock Gavin and Edward strolled in, immaculate in the satin knee breeches that were required evening dress for gentlemen. Edward was not a habitué of Almack's but like Gavin he had come to offer any support Carina might need in her debut. It was readily apparent that she stood in no desperate need as she whirled past them with no time for more than a smile in passing. She did enjoy a dance with Edward shortly afterward. The disparity in height made Edward a somewhat awkward partner for Carina, but as it never occurred to her to wonder what people might be thinking of her appearance when she was engaged in a pleasurable activity, she allowed nothing to blight the comfortable feeling she always experienced in Edward's company. She chatted away unself-consciously, describing to him the people she had met.

There was another waltz toward the end of the evening and once again Carina found herself sought after by her handsome new acquaintance, Lord Edgemere. He put himself out to be entertaining, and such was his address that he succeeded very well with a young lady who was already becoming known for her dislike of formal gallantry.

Gavin Delawney, glancing around from the sofa where he was participating in a light flirtation with Lady Jersey who frankly enjoyed audacious young men, heard the waltz music strike up and wondered with amusement whether the irrepressible Carina would be able to conceal her chagrin at being obliged to forgo dancing. He spotted her engaged in what had every appearance of a most enjoyable tête-à-tête. He was about to beg Lady Jersey's pardon for his momentary inattention when the identity of Carina's companion impressed itself forcibly upon him and a ferocious scowl marred his countenance fleetingly. It was gone in an instant and his voice was completely controlled as he remarked:

"This is a new start for Guy Accrington, is it not? Almack's has not been honored by his presence above twice in the half-dozen years I have known him."

No one could have gleaned from his casual tone that he was seething inwardly, but Lady Jersey had noted the black look and the direction of his glance. No one had ever accused her of being slow of comprehension, and her facile brain was writhing with amused conjecture as she answered him just as casually.

"Ah, but that was before he succeeded in running through what little money the late earl was possessed of when he died two years ago. The new earl gets his good looks from his mother, but his propensity for expensive horses and more expensive women is inherited directly from his father."

Gavin snorted. "If he is hanging out for a rich wife, he is dangling after the wrong Raven sister; Carina hasn't a bean."

Since Lady Jersey was well aware that Mr. Delawney had been, if not dangling precisely, at least most attentive to the Raven heiress himself, she was a bit surprised by this remark, but not for anything would she have displayed her curiosity as to why the gentleman's usual *sang-froid* had been so disturbed by the sight of the Earl of Edgemere making himself agreeable to the ingenuous young sister of the heiress. For a moment he had looked murderous, a most unusual departure from his customary careless good humor. She merely said with synthetic sweetness:

"The little Raven is attractive enough to catch the eye of a connoisseur and no one could deny that Guy Accrington is a connoisseur of women. I witnessed their initial meeting earlier and it was obvious that he was greatly *épris* with her charms."

Gavin had his distaste for the situation under cool control now. "When has Edgemere ever displayed any interest in pretty innocents? He prefers 'em ripe and knowledgeable."

"The right woman can change a man's habits, do you not agree?"

Far from agreeing with this mawkish sentiment, Gavin disagreed strongly but forbore to argue. Instead he smiled with great charm at his hostess.

"It will do the chit no good at all to have her

name linked with a womanizer like Edgemere. Will you permit me to get her away from him by asking her to dance, ma'am?"

This instance of the pot calling the kettle black strongly appealed to Lady Jersey's sense of the ridiculous, as did the image of Gavin Delawney, the scourge of the matchmaking mamas, rescuing a young girl's reputation, but she concealed her malicious appreciation under a thoughtful demeanor and rose gracefully from the sofa.

"Perhaps you are right," she said with assumed gravity, placing her hand on his arm and allowing herself to be led to the nook where Carina was still engrossed in conversation with the object of their discussion.

"Miss Raven, you do not dance. May I present Mr. Gavin Delawney as a most desirable partner in the waltz?"

Carina looked up in surprise. She had not even been aware of their approach and now glanced doubtfully from Lady Jersey to the two men, unsure of what she should do.

Lady Jersey took charge. "You do waltz, Miss Raven?"

Carina's chin with its tiny center dent went up a trifle. "Of course, ma'am," she said politely to Lady Jersey. As she took Gavin's extended hand she smiled apologetically at the earl. "If you will excuse me, my lord?"

"Most reluctantly, Miss Carina. I will console myself with the expectation of waltzing with you myself the next time we meet."

Carina's dimples shone through in the bare second before Gavin had whirled her away for what remained of the waltz. At first she simply gave herself up to the pleasure of moving in absolute harmony with a magnificent partner to the exquisitely beautiful Viennese music. At the sound of Gavin's soft laugh, however, she raised her eyes in mute question.

"You look as if the music had cast a spell over you," he said by way of explanation.

Carina smiled, though her face still retained a somewhat dreamy expression. "I think it has. However did you accomplish this, Gavin? I quite feared I'd have to wait weeks for permission to waltz. I think you must be what Tony calls a complete hand."

"If I thought Tony Mercer was corrupting your pure accents, little one, I would declare him an unfit companion for you, but since your vocabulary has no doubt been alarmingly increased by years of stable boys' company I shall refrain from censoring Tony."

"You have not answered my question," said Carina, prudently ignoring this thrust. She was feeling too deliciously alive to wish to quarrel with Gavin tonight.

"How we come to be waltzing? You owe it all to my polished address, my dear," he declared modestly.

Carina gave him a wicked look from under those black eyelashes. "Is that what one calls flirting with older women—address? I must remember that."

"Quiet brat, just dance. I have no intention, on the dance floor, of indulging your liking for quarreling." He pulled her a degree closer and she subsided with a tiny chuckle, retreating to her earlier reverie.

He looked measuringly at her rapt face from time to time, wondering what he should say if she chanced to mention her erstwhile companion, but he need not have concerned himself with this unlikely possibility, for Carina was utterly content to be dancing so smoothly, and in Gavin's company she never gave a thought to other people anyway.

Nor did she realize that they were attracting a deal of attention from the dowagers seated around the room. Gavin Delawney was certainly a matrimonial prize but so slippery that all but the most determined mothers of unwed daughters had reluctantly abandoned the chase. It was not an unusual sight to see him directing his considerable charm at the prettiest girl at any gathering, but since his propensity for switching his attentions before any young lady's parents could begin to hope he might be serious was well known, it was not the fact of his devoting himself to Carina Raven but rather the somewhat spectacular picture of those two fiery heads together that drew attention. None but the most jealous of hopeful mamas could deny they presented a most appealing picture of grace, vitality and sparkling good looks.

Lady Jersey, who was not one of the jealous mamas, was fully able to appreciate the charming picture the effortlessly twirling couple made. Her expression was thoughtful and became even more so as she noted Elizabeth Raven smiling at her sister as she caught Carina's eye as the dance ended. Gavin brought his laughing partner to a theatrical whirling halt before her sister and the three remained chattering animatedly until both girls were claimed by their next partners.

Lady Jersey regarded Gavin's straight back with new interest as he headed toward the card room. He and the little Raven girl undoubtedly made a handsome pair, but then so did he and Elizabeth. However, Elizabeth Raven, with her fortune, would have her pick of all the eligible and most of the ineligible males, while dowerless Carina, for all her current popularity, could not be expected to contract more than a respectable alliance unless a wealthy man just happened to fall head over ears in love with her. Obviously Gavin Delawney felt quite ridiculously protective of the child already. Lady Jersey was intrigued but not as yet prepared to postulate whether this was due to his admiration for Elizabeth or to some unacknowledged feelings for the younger girl. Decidedly that three-cornered friendship would bear watching.

Lady Jersey would have found the tea party at the Raven household two afternoons later productive ground for watching developments if she had chanced to call. The same cast of players was present with the addition of Sir Edward Lynton who had been persuaded to join Gavin after a session at Jackson's in hopes of finding the ladies at home and receiving. Gavin, who suspected Ned of cherishing a secret *tendre* for Carina, was rather surprised at his friend's obvious reluctance to accompany him but rode roughshod over his hesitant attempts to withdraw gracefully. They were happily making enormous inroads on Cook's delicious cheese tarts in an effort to replenish the energy expended in fisticuffs when the Earl of Edgemere was announced.

"So she can blush after all," Gavin noted

silently but wrathfully, and barely kept his disgust hidden as he alone remarked the faint color stealing over Carina's creamy skin. However, even such an unreasoning critic could find no fault with Carina's manner toward the earl as the afternoon wore on. She treated him with the same gay friendliness she displayed toward most of the males of her acquaintance. Nor did she respond to the particularity to herself displayed within the bounds of good manners by the earl. In fact, Gavin reluctantly admitted, she revealed a social talent for keeping the conversation entertaining and of general interest that he would never have suspected in one so inexperienced.

"By the way, Miss Carina," interposed the earl at a moment when Miss Silverdown was engaging the attention of the rest of the party with an anecdote relating to her late father's pilgrimages to the Newmarket races, "I understand you are particularly fond of riding. I would be most grateful if you would consent to try the paces of a pretty little mare I have just purchased for my sister's use and give me your opinion of her suitability as a lady's mount." The earl paused briefly and looked inquiringly at Carina whose face clearly reflected her willingness to oblige. He went on without giving her a chance to speak. "Unfortunately, I have a previous engagement tomorrow. Do you happen to be free Friday afternoon?"

Before Carina could open her mouth to voice her acceptance of the invitation, she heard Gavin's smooth tones declining for her:

"So sorry, old chap, but you are just a bit too late. I had just made arrangements to ride with

Carina on Friday afternoon. Better luck next time."

He was wearing a blandly sympathetic expression, but Carina, whose startled eyes had flown to his at the beginning of this outrageously untruthful speech, saw the dancing devils in the blue depths and she itched to slap him soundly for his officious interference in her affairs.

The earl's eyes had narrowed slightly at Gavin's announcement and he turned to Carina for confirmation.

There was the tiniest hesitation and then Carina said in regretful tones, "I am so sorry." She felt rather than saw the slight relaxation in Gavin's body where he lounged in a rather casual attitude beside her on the sofa, and she shot him a cold look before adding with an exaggerated wistfulness and a wholly ingratiating smile for the earl: "I would love to try your mare another time if it would be convenient?" She allowed a questioning note to creep into her voice and was pleased at the sudden scowl that briefly marred Gavin's satisfied countenance.

"I will be away for several days next week but as soon as I return I will call if I may to arrange a time."

Carina smiled her consent at the earl and the conversation became general once again. Although she was determined to be private with Gavin for long enough to demand an explanation of his conduct, he blindly ignored her signaling eye and casually took his leave, accompanying Sir Edward and the earl downstairs to the street where they found themselves walking in the same direction for a time. The earl was conversing with determined amiability in the face of Edward's civil indifference and Gavin's air of preoccupation. Eventually he returned to the people they had just left.

"Do you ride often with Miss Raven, Miss Carina Raven, I should say?" he inquired at last of Gavin with the air of one trying to establish a basis for conversation.

"Yes," Gavin answered baldly.

Edward stepped into the breech left by this non sequitur.

"You will find in Carina an excellent rider," he said politely. "I've yet to see the horse she cannot manage."

"She is an extremely lovely girl too," remarked the earl, glancing quickly at Gavin. "In my experience heiresses have always had either a squint or spots or a positive hump, but those two girls are quite beautiful."

"Quite, but in the interests of accuracy I feel I should point out that only one of them is an heiress," put in Gavin laconically.

The earl raised an eyebrow in a face that had become a polite social mask, but the other men sensed his quickened interest. Neither chose to amplify Gavin's statement, however, and finally the earl ventured:

"It is widely rumored, certainly, that the Raven sisters are considerable heiresses. Does rumor lie, then?"

"Not in the case of Elizabeth Raven," answered Sir Edward. "She was the principal heir to old Lord Silverdown's private fortune."

"And Miss Carina Raven?"

"I have no certain knowledge of the provisions

Matthew Raven may have made for his younger daughter."

"Matthew Raven? Is he her father? Then I should think it would be safe to say her portion would depend on how his horses place at Newmarket." The earl laughed and Gavin barely restrained a strong urge to choke him lifeless.

"But, as you remarked earlier, Carina is a lovely girl. Her beauty and charm are in no way dependent on how her father's horses place." His voice was smooth but those startling blue eyes glinted challengingly.

Edward sent him a warmly approving look and the earl hastily averred his complete agreement with this sentiment, then as they had reached the corner of Bond Street, he took his leave of them with well-concealed relief.

"I hope Carina will not be too disappointed not to try the mare," commented Gavin dryly.

"Oh, she'll ride with him next week."

Gavin turned on his quiet-faced friend with something approaching snarling fury. "If you think to convince me Edgemere is other than a gilt-edged fortune hunter you may save your breath. His type would never be seriously interested in a baby like Carina."

"Carina is not the baby you think her, my friend, but enough of that. She'll convince you of that far more effectively than I." The slight smile flickering over Edward's impassive features fired Gavin with a brief impulse to draw his cork, but Edward raised a placating hand and continued:

"Edgemere's too clever to cancel out a prearranged appointment. He's a fortune hunter all right, but Carina was never in real jeopardy because he was bound to discover the truth soon. Besides she's too shrewd to form a *tendre* for a block of ice like the pretty earl. No, Elizabeth is the one in danger from Edgemere—she *does* possess a fortune."

Gavin wondered at the hint of bitterness in his friend's voice but thought him overly concerned. He said carefully:

"Elizabeth Raven does not strike me as impressionable; indeed the opposite would be nearer the truth. There is an air of cool reserve about her that tells a man in no uncertain terms that he has not touched her heart."

"The fact that she does not seem to ... to form emotional attachments is what makes me fear Edgemere's influence. She is past twenty and must be considering it time to marry—at least so Carina has hinted. If there is no question of affection involved, who could appear to more advantage than Edgemere? He is handsome, intelligent and no one can deny he knows how to make himself agreeable to women, not to mention the lure of the title. Most girls would jump at the chance to become a countess."

Gavin could not logically rebut any of Ned's arguments, but his instincts prompted his serious answer.

"Somehow I do not believe Elizabeth Raven to be among their number."

Edward's face was a closed book to his friend, but he returned no answer and the two parted company at the corner of St. James's Street.

CHAPTER 6

Carina regarded the closed door with acute indignation.

"Well, did you see that?" She addressed her relatives impartially. "He *knew* I wanted an explanation and he simply left!"

Elizabeth smiled sympathetically.

Miss Silverdown said dryly, "You are discovering that there is no animal so elusive as a male human who does not wish to be questioned by the females of his acquaintance."

Carina laughed but she was puzzled too. "The other evening at Almack's Tony made some sly reference to the earl's reputation but later when I asked him what he meant he fobbed me off and changed the subject. And now Gavin jumps in to prevent my riding with the earl, then refuses to explain why he acted thusly. I am quite out of charity with him," she finished crossly and her soft mouth was set in a stubborn line.

"Yet I notice you did not overturn his ploy by denying you had a previous engagement which was no more than the truth," Elizabeth suggested slyly.

Now Carina's indignation was directed toward her sister.

"But, Liza, you know I could not do such a thing to Gavin in front of the earl."

An enigmatic little smile hovered around Elizabeth's lips.

"No?"

"Well, of course not! The earl is the merest acquaintance. I could not embarrass Gavin in his presence."

"Gavin Delawney being an old friend of at least three weeks' standing," said Miss Silverdown with gentle mockery.

Elizabeth laughed but said soothingly, "Never mind, Dearest, you shall not be teased about your commendable loyalty to Gavin or his ... protectiveness toward you."

For a moment Carina's face wore a faintly troubled expression. "Liza," she said hesitantly, "you know Gavin treats me like a young sister, do you not? It is you he has a *tendre* for."

"Has he?" With this noncommittal reply Elizabeth brought the conversation to a somewhat unsatisfactory conclusion as far as her sister was concerned and returned to her bedchamber to change, leaving Carina to ponder over the inexplicable behavior of Gavin and her sister, not to mention Tony Mercer the other evening. What was the mystery about the Earl of Edgemere?

She was no wiser after her ride with Gavin on Friday, for he merely defended his own behavior by claiming the earl had just beaten him to the punch with his invitation and he had acted on the impulse of the moment in claiming a prior engagement. Carina did not for a minute believe this tale and was decidedly cool to him during their ride but was not granted the satisfaction of seeing his tearing spirits affected to the least degree. It took all her determination not to let herself be carried along on the wave of his cheerfulness, but she felt she owed it to herself to remain aloof. In the last moment before parting, she thought she saw a rather rueful gleam in his eyes as he expressed a wish that their next meeting would be more amicable, and although she cautioned herself not to jump to the probably erroneous conclusion that he valued her good opinion, she was slightly comforted and bestowed her first warm smile of the day on him. It was a tremendous effort for Carina to remember she was displeased with someone, so it was with considerable relief that she abandoned her haughty attitude.

It was not from Gavin but her friend Sir Anthony Mercer that she finally received information concerning her new admirer. Tony was not quite so experienced as Gavin in keeping determined females at bay. She took him roundly to task during a dance at the Sefton's ball. It was a very warm evening and the rooms were greatly overcrowded. Carina and Sir Anthony were sitting out a dance, cosily but too warmly ensconced on a green satin sofa in an alcove that was miraculously deserted for the moment. Sir Anthony was lazily fanning Carina with her charming gilt and enamel fan when she suddenly sat upright and fixed her amiable companion with an accusing eye.

"Tony, I wish to know what you meant the other night when you told Lord Edgemere I did not yet know of his reputation."

Sir Anthony shifted uneasily on the sofa and a vague expression came across his face. "Don't think I recall the incident," he muttered. "Don't really know much about Edgemere—don't travel in the same circles, you know."

"Tony," Carina began warningly.

"Must have been slightly on the go that night, likely to say anything—a lot of nonsense—in that condition, you know."

"Oh, Tony, you idiot," gasped Carina, laughing at his faintly hunted expression. "Foxed at Almack's? On ratafia, no doubt. I am not so green as to swallow that." She added in a wheedling tone, "I particularly wish to know because the earl called on us shortly afterward and invited me to go riding with him. There was another gentleman present at the time and he pretended we already had a prior engagement so I had to refuse the earl's invitation."

"Did he really? Well, stands to reason—a man like Edgemere and a young girl—wouldn't do at all."

Carina's clear gray eyes were huge and questioning.

"Tony, is Lord Edgemere not a respectable person for me to know? He was presented to my sister last year and I met him at Almack's, after all."

"It ain't so much that he's not respectable, although for my part that's a moot point, but his taste in women don't usually run to fledgling debutantes." He squirmed on the seat and put a finger inside his collar to ease the tightness of his wilted shirt points.

Carina nodded knowledgeably:

"Ah, I understand. He prefers the muslin company and fast widows."

Sir Anthony uttered a strangled exclamation.

"Carina," he begged, "please, for my sake, don't say I told you any such thing. It ain't the thing for girls your age to know about such women."

"Oh, pooh, what is the sense of sticking one's head in the sand like an ostrich?" As Sir Anthony's color went from red to pale purple, she relented and patted his arm soothingly. "Don't fash yourself, lad, as my old Yorkshire-born nurse was used to say. I will not mention the bits of muslin or light-skirts or opera dancers in company." His color faded somewhat but the mischievous look in her eyes brought back the hunted look to his, and he sought desperately for a change of subject. Carina sat thoughtfully while he bungled about for a moment, then said abruptly.

"But, Tony, if Lord Edgemere prefers the mus . . . women of a different type," she amended at his look of anguish, "why is he displaying an interest in me?"

Sir Anthony coughed and stared at some point over her left shoulder. "It's said he's all to pieces, must marry money, that's why he's been frequenting Almack's just lately."

"I have no fortune at all," Carina protested.

"Your sister does," he pointed out.

"Yes, of course, but I am the one he has singled out," she said with a puckered brow. "Ah, well, all shall become clear in time no doubt." She indicated that they should return to the ballroom, and Sir Anthony, glad to terminate one of the more uncomfortable conversations it had ever been his misfortune to become entrapped in, jumped to his feet and offered her his arm.

"Just the same," he told her with unusual seriousness, "it wouldn't do to form a *tendre* for a man of Edgemere's stamp."

"Oh, no, you may be sure I will not." She gave a reminiscent little shudder. "One look at those cold eyes was enough to warn me that he would make the very devil of a husband." A sharp nip on her arm warned her that once again she was indulging in language unbecoming to a girl of her tender years and she subsided, composing her features to the appearance of a slightly mischievous choirboy as Tony led her to her next partner.

Tony's disclosures had heightened Carina's interest in the Earl of Edgemere, and when he sent a note requesting a convenient time to ride together, she answered immediately and found herself looking forward eagerly to their imminent meeting. In the event, however, the ride proved disappointing, not because of the lovely gray mare who proved to be a very well-behaved lady's hack, but due to the earl's attitude which had veered from that of a potential suitor past the avuncular, all the way to the paternal. He was affable in the extreme and careful of her comfort, but with such an air of one indulging a young child that Carina's hackles rose although she managed to conceal her surprise and chagrin under an amused pose of civility. He was all eagerness to discuss Elizabeth it seemed and set gently afloat the implication that he hoped Carina would stand his friend with her sister.

Carina was not a conceited girl, but neither was she stupid. Far from expecting men to fall at her feet, she had been astonished and, if the truth be known, a bit alarmed to find herself so sought after, but she was not so inexperienced as to fail to

spot the difference in the earl's present attitude
from that displayed in their previous encounters.
She knew he was trying to leave the impression
that he had looked on her as a pretty child from
the first, and she felt nothing but contempt for his
performance, although she endeavored to conceal
this, partly from good manners, but mainly because she wished to discover his game if he had
one and did not desire to put herelf at a disad-
vantage.

It did not take a classical scholar to unravel his
motives in pretending his earlier interest in Carina had been that of a would-be brother rather
than a suitor. From the time of their ride together
the earl devoted himself to a single-minded pursuit of her sister that utterly convinced Carina
that Tony had indeed told her no more than the
truth about their noble admirer's status as a
gazetted fortune hunter. She had a keen appreciation for the irony of his having defeated his own
purpose by his attempted deception of herself.
Carina had always believed the greater portion of
the masculine population must of necessity fall in
love with her beautiful and lovable sister. If the
earl had not taken such pains to persuade the
younger girl that any previous attentions to herself were in the nature of campaign strategy to
win Elizabeth's favor, she would simply have assumed he had felt a brief attraction for herself
that had been submerged in the deeper pull of
Elizabeth's attraction.

The earl's frequent calls in Green Street perforce were a source of great annoyance to Carina,
who found it difficult to suppress a feeling of repugnance at the sight of his debonairly smiling

face. On the first few occasions she anxiously studied her sister's reaction, but since Elizabeth seemed not to distinguish the earl from any of her other suitors, she allowed herself to relax and decided it would not be necessary to mention Tony's revelations to her aunt or sister.

Carina continued to have a merry time over the next few weeks, although when she had a spare moment to consider, she realized with a little pang that they had seen much less of Gavin and Edward recently. Gavin kindly invited her to ride with him about once a week, and on these happy occasions he treated her in the same breezy, companionable fashion as before, but his calls on the ladies had lessened. They did not meet Edward above twice during this interval, and that accidentally at assemblies. He did not once come to Green Street, and at last Carina mentioned this omission to her sister when they were alone in the small sitting room one morning.

"Liza, do you suppose Edward has been ill? We have seen almost nothing of him of late."

Elizabeth did not look up from her fingers which were busy tightening her embroidery frame. Her voice was quiet.

"I do not believe so. I caught a glimpse of him at Lady Ogilvie's drum last night."

"Did you? I did not see him at all. Did he come up to you?"

"No." There was an infinitesimal pause then Elizabeth proceeded, "He seemed surrounded by quite a number of friends and may not have noticed me at all." She asked Carina's help in sorting her silks then and the subject was allowed to drop.

It reoccurred forcibly to Carina a few days later, however, when she witnessed a strange tableau at an evening party. She was approaching a group which included her sister when she noticed Edward in the distance staring fixedly at Elizabeth's profile. At about that time Elizabeth turned slowly in his direction. Instantly Edward's gaze shifted and he proceeded to move away at a slow pace. Carina was astonished at the expression of real pain that flashed across her sister's face before she turned, smiling once again, back to her companions.

Carina stopped short, an unthinking rage against Edward rising in her breast. He had all but given Elizabeth the cut direct. She had been so engrossed with Elizabeth's reaction she had not noticed where Edward had gone, but now she began a systematic search of the rooms looking for him. He was not going to escape without explaining his extraordinary behavior toward one of his oldest friends. Her vivacious little face reflected her cold determination a few moments later when she spied Edward heading toward a cloakroom and she took a couple of running steps while calling out to him,

"Edward, wait please."

At the sound of her voice he turned and approached her, smiling affectionately. "Hello, my dear, how are you?"

Her footsteps halted and she gazed at him in bewilderment.

"Edward, is something wrong?"

"Of course not, what could be wrong?" His tone was normal, but Carina's searching eyes found his slightly evasive.

"You are looking very charming tonight. That sea green confection becomes you."

The compliment appeared to distress rather than please Carina. She lifted an imploring hand and let it drop.

"Edward, I saw you a few moments ago when you were looking at Liza. When she turned toward you, you turned away, it seemed purposely. Liza was hurt. I watched her." She paused, her eyes never leaving his face that had grown very still until she mentioned Elizabeth's pain, and then she thought she detected an echo of this in his eyes.

"Edward, what is it? Have we offended you in some way?"

He absentmindedly covered the anxious little hand on his sleeve with one of his and leveled burning eyes on the girl beside him.

"Carina, you have always stood my friend. Surely you must realize how difficult it is for me to meet Elizabeth. You are not too young to understand my feelings."

She looked stunned. "What feelings? Why should it be difficult for you to meet Liza? I do not understand you."

Now he looked at her uncomprehendingly. "Do you mean she has never told you?"

"Told me what? Edward, stop being so mysterious."

He shook his head slowly. "No, Carina, if Elizabeth has not told you, then I do not feel I should go against her wishes. We will leave it, my dear."

"Oh, no, we will not!" she exclaimed mutinously. "If you do not tell me at once, Edward, I promise you I shall repeat this conversation to

Liza in its entirety and ask her for an explanation." Determination was visible in every rigid
line of her graceful body.

Gray eyes met hazel ones challengingly and at
last the hazel eyes fell. "Very well," he said tone-
lessly. "There is no great mystery. Two years ago
I asked your father's permission to pay my
addresses to Elizabeth and he refused. That is all
there is to it, but now perhaps you can appreciate
why it is difficult for me to be continuously meeting Elizabeth at social gatherings such as this."

The clear gray eyes were misty with unshed
tears.

"I am so sorry, Edward. You still love her." It
was not a question.

"I always shall," he replied simply.

"Edward, why don't you try again? Liza has
not formed a *tendre* for anyone else, of that I am
sure."

His features hardened. "No, Carina, your father
thought me a poor prospect two years ago even
before Elizabeth inherited your grandfather's
money. Do you honestly imagine he would look
with more favor on my suit now? A mere baronet
when Elizabeth can have her pick of the wealthy
and titled?"

Carina frowned. "How does Elizabeth feel? Did
she wish to marry you two years ago?"

He hesitated. "I do not know. At that time I
thought perhaps she was not entirely indifferent
to me, but she was very young. I did not see her
for some time afterward."

Carina recalled that Edward had begun to
spend much more time in London about then and
they had seen much less of him over the past two

years. How stupid she had been not to guess! But Edward was such a gentleman, he had concealed his feelings too well.

He went on evenly: "Your grandfather died about then, delaying Elizabeth's come-out you will remember. When we met again in town last year, she was her old self at first, as though nothing had changed between us." He frowned slightly and proceeded with some difficulty. "Gradually, though, I have sensed a coldness creeping into her manner toward me." He straightened up and his face became calm and empty again. "No, Carina, it is a closed issue; Elizabeth has no feeling for me other than friendship."

Carina gazed at him with deep compassion. Poor Edward—she longed to comfort him, to help him if possible, but for the moment she was at a loss. Impulsively she squeezed his hand in wordless sympathy and Edward directed the warmth of his rare smile at her.

It was at this precise moment that Elizabeth approached on the arm of a young fashionable dressed in the extreme style of the dedicated dandy. Carina's awed glance played over his wasp-waisted coat and its platter-sized buttons, but Elizabeth's eyes were on her sister and their old friend. She had halted rather abruptly some few feet away and she remained silent, her lovely face a careful blank. Carina, sensing the sudden tension in the air, dragged her fascinated gaze from the embroidered waistcoat of her sister's escort and plunged into speech with forced cheerfulness in a praiseworthy attempt to ease the situation.

"I was just saying good night to Edward who

must leave early unfortunately," she intoned rather breathlessly.

Edward's quiet voice followed her lead. "Yes, I fear I was promised to some friends at Brooks's a good half hour ago."

Carina could not tell whether this apologetic explanation served to ease the sense of mortification Elizabeth must have experienced at Edward's earlier behavior. Her sister merely inclined her head politely and said with her easy social grace:

"Then pray do not let us detain you any longer. Your friends must be aware that punctuality is one of your virtues; they will begin to worry at the delay. Good night, Edward."

"Good night, Elizabeth, Carina." With a formal bow that included the three of them Edward was gone.

For the first time ever there was some constraint between the sisters on the ride home that evening. By then Carina had had time to assimulate Edward's startling announcement and to realize the enormity of the fact that Liza had never confided so much as a hint of the situation to her. A far closer bond existed between the sisters than obtained in most families, and before tonight she would have had no hesitation in saying she and Liza shared their innermost thoughts. To say she was shaken in this certainty could only be a grave understatement. Carina sat silent and curiously vulnerable in the carriage, heedless of the intent glances her sister sent her way from time to time. Twice Elizabeth seemed about to utter some remark but appeared to change her mind and remained as silent as her sister except that she made polite though brief replies to Miss Silverdown's queries as to their experiences that evening. Carina was so engrossed with her unpleasant musings that she appeared completely unaware of her companions and eventually her uncharacteristic silence came to the attention of her aunt who would certainly have inquired as to the reasons had the carriage not drawn up to the door at that moment. As it was she contented herself with detaining Elizabeth to question her about her sister's quietness. Elizabeth made evasive but apparently satisfactory replies and the two ladies headed upstairs together a few moments after Carina.

Had her sister not stopped to talk with Miss Silverdown, thus momentarily delaying her retirement to her bedchamber, it is probable Carina would have repeated Edward's revelations to her and demanded to know why she had never thought to mention the affair. By the next morning, however, she had had several restless hours in which to ponder the situation and had reluctantly arrived at a decision to maintain the silence on the subject that had existed for two years. Although very hurt by her sister's failure to confide in her, she felt she had no choice but to respect her reserve. After all, Elizabeth might have disclosed the situation any time these past two years but had elected to remain silent. Mulling over her sister's recent and past behavior in her mind, she realized that she did not have a clue as to whether her father's refusal to consider Edward's suit had disappointed Elizabeth or not. Certainly she had noticed that Liza had become more self-contained since her first season in town and lost some of her glowing enthusiasm for new experiences, but that could be simply explained as the natural result of conforming to the behavior expected of a newly launched debutante. She simply could not reconcile Liza's cheerful serenity with a broken heart however well concealed.

If, as seemed likely, her sister had not cared deeply for Edward two years ago, how did she feel about him today? Had she grown cold as Edward feared—was his occasional presence an uncomfortable reminder that she had been unable to return his affection? Casting her mind back over the last few weeks in town, Carina rather thought that Liza never spoke of Edward voluntarily but when she did discuss him there was no hint of rebuke or antipathy in her manner. She came to the reluctant decision that any well-meant interference on her part would only serve to exacerbate the delicate balance. Much as she longed to help Edward, under the circumstances it would be sheer cruelty to expose him to more of Elizabeth's society than he had to endure in accidental meetings.

In her preoccupation with Edward's unrequited love, she had not once thought of Gavin whose suit she had been actively supporting until now. The knowledge that she could no longer be unreservedly delighted if Gavin won her sister's hand caused her to sigh deeply, but she resolutely put all thoughts of the unhappy situation out of her mind in preparation for greeting her sister and aunt. The one action that was demanded of her, it seemed, was that most trying one of pretending continued ignorance before Liza. Everything must appear as before. For the first time since their arrival in London, she faced the day's pleasures with some reluctance as she left her bedchamber at last.

CHAPTER 7

Although Carina tried hard there were subtle changes in the atmosphere in Green Street following that fateful talk with Edward. She felt Elizabeth watching her more closely and found herself weighing her words before speaking. In her sister's company she sometimes was less natural than among her newest acquaintances and this disturbed her. She realized she was rather avoiding Liza at times and hoped desperately that her sister did not guess this.

For her part Elizabeth had an air of expecting some confidence from her sister. Several times she seemed on the brink of questioning her about her feelings and once she actually did ask Carina rather urgently if she was quite happy with their activities and begged her to come to her sister if any situation should arise that troubled her. This confrontation left Carina utterly bewildered, but she hoped she had convinced her sister of her contentment with their life.

One situation that did arise that troubled Carina was the gradual change in the status of her sister's noble admirer. In the last week or so Elizabeth had begun to demonstrate a slight but decided preference for the earl's company. Before this she had remained resolutely impartial toward her army of suitors, but now she began to distinguish the earl by agreeing more often to his suggestions for pleasure outings than to any others. Edgemere was present at almost every assembly and ball to which the sisters were invited and lost no time in making his way to Elizabeth's side. She could not possibly dance with every man who sought her hand during an evening, but Edgemere was never among the disappointed lookers-on. In their inevitable encounters he treated Carina with a sham friendliness that those cold eyes denied. With Elizabeth, his pose of love-struck pretendant to her hand was perfection except for those same eyes that never warmed entirely. His presence grated on Carina's nerves, and after one call where she had taken refuge in stiff civility from his veiled mockery, she pounced on her sister the moment Miss Silverdown left the room to change for dinner.

"Liza, have you . . . that is, do you . . .?" Somehow it was much more difficult than she had imagined to broach the subject of her sister's feelings toward the earl. Elizabeth was looking at her expectantly. She took a deep breath and began again: "Have you formed a *tendre* for Lord Edgemere?"

Elizabeth's face remained serenely composed. "If I have, how would you feel about it?" she asked calmly.

Carina swallowed convulsively as her worst fears seemed about to come true, but plunged bravely on. "Tony told me Lord Edgemere has lost all his fortune and must marry money." She paused to watch her sister's reaction, but she was not prepared for the matter-of-fact reply.

"Yes, I am aware that Edgemere has joined the ranks of the fortune hunters."

"And you do not care—that he does not love you, I mean?" Carina was aghast at Elizabeth's acceptance of the situation.

"Do you know that he does not?" Her sister looked merely interested, not upset.

"His eyes give him away," Carina said promptly. "They would instantly freeze water. I would willingly wager my nonexistent fortune that Guy Accrington is utterly incapable of the more tender emotions. He is courting you solely for your possessions. Tony says he is notorious for preferring a low class of women."

"Tony seems to be a font of information about Edgemere," was the dry response. "Well, I'll not attempt to argue with such heartfelt conviction. How should I indeed, when I am well accustomed to being wooed for the sake of my fortune?"

"Liza!" Carina protested, disturbed by the hint of bitterness in her sister's voice. "Many of your suitors have been completely sincere in their protestations of affection. Sir John Macaulay was quite crushed when you refused him. He positively languishes when you meet in public."

"Sir John derives a good deal of comfort from his public pose of rejected lover. I believe he fancies himself a poet and poets thrive on sorrow, you know."

"Liza, how cruel! I truly believe his affection for you is real."

Elizabeth abandoned her attempt to speak lightly and studied her young sister's troubled face. "Real perhaps, but not deeply felt, my dear.

How could it be when we were scarcely acquainted? It pleased Sir John to put me on a pedestal to adore from afar. He made little effort to really know me. It is, regrettably, rather the fashion to be in worshipful attendance on Miss Elizabeth Raven this year. No doubt it will soon pass and some other lady will be similarly honored."

"You sound very cynical; it is not like you."

"Do I? I am sorry, Dearest, but I grow weary of the situation. Do you not think it is time I decided to settle down? At least Edgemere is extremely personable, intelligent, and you must grant his appearance is enough to cause a flutter in any girl's heart."

"Has he fluttered yours?" Carina asked gravely, her honest gray eyes searching her sister's face.

Elizabeth wore that closed look again. "I fear I must be one of those cold females who is constitutionally unable to form a deep attachment," she declared lightly. "Now let us proceed to more interesting matters. What gown do you plan to wear to the theater tonight?" She chuckled softly. "I think I shall wear red since Edgemere is said to favor a slightly more dashing style of female." She glanced brightly at Carina who ignored the challenge in the blue eyes. She accepted the fact that the subject was closed but went upstairs to dress deeply distressed. In the last fifteen minutes her beloved sister had become almost a stranger. Although she would not credit the essentially gentle and kind Elizabeth with believing the worldly sentiments she had so recently expressed, she was wholly at a loss to comprehend why her sister should wish to create this false impression.

Never had she looked forward with less enthusiasm to a visit to the theater. At any other time the prospect of witnessing the great Kean play Shylock would have thrilled her to the marrow, but they were going in a party of the earl's instigation, and, after the afternoon tea just endured, she was reluctant to put her good manners to a further test. Her mind dwelling on the annoyance of several additional hours in the earl's company, she failed to realize the force which her agitated thoughts were lending to the hand wielding a hairbrush until a particularly savage stroke brought sudden tears of pain to her eyes. Flicking a look into the mirror she discovered her short locks were standing out from her head in wild disorder. Her petulant expression vanished as she giggled.

"If the play was *Macbeth* instead of the *Merchant of Venice* you should fit right into the first scene," she solemnly assured the looking-glass image.

It was necessary to dampen her wild hair slightly before she was able to restore it to its usual soft curls. In the end she was happy to accept Abby's help in arraying herself in a becoming jonquil silk gown. She snatched up a matching cloak, seized her reticule and opera glasses from Abby's hand and began her dash down the stairs just as the footman dispatched to inquire as to her lateness reached the halfway point. She grinned at him cheerfully.

"It's all right, Michael, here I am."

Gradually, during the course of a delicious dinner, Carina recovered her usual equable disposition and by the time the earl called for the ladies and assisted them tenderly into his luxurious car-

riage, she was beginning to indulge a cautious
optimism as to the possibility of spending an
enjoyable evening even in the company of the detestably patronizing earl. This optimism was reinforced when she discovered Sir Anthony Mercer
was to be among the party as well as General
Worcester, an old friend of Miss Silverdown's.

And during the greater portion of the excellent
production, she did enjoy herself thoroughly. Carina had only been to the theater on two previous
occasions and she was the perfect spectator, attentive and responsive, sitting in rapt silence
while the actors displayed their art. During the
intervals their box was the scene of a lively reception as members of Elizabeth's court crowded in
to pay their respects. There was a spirited discussion of the temerity shown by Edmund Kean in
discarding the traditional red wig in which Shylock
had been portrayed for uncounted years. The
traffic in the box was such that Carina was easily
able to ignore the earl's presence without giving
offense while she concentrated her friendly attentions on Tony Mercer. In any case, the earl, as
host, was devoting his attention to his elder guests
and to keeping the traffic around Elizabeth moving.

The incident that distinguished the evening in
Carina's memory did not occur until late in the
play when for the moment the original party remained alone in the box. Tony, who had been
saying nothing in particular with his usual gay
camaraderie, broke off in the middle of a sentence:

"I say, almost forgot. They are holding a
masquerade at the Pantheon Thursday. Should
you and your sister like to attend, do you think?

It will be a lively affair, not much like Almack's."

"Oh, Tony, what a delightful idea! I've heard the Pantheon rooms are most impressively decorated. I should like very much to go. Do they wear historical costume or just dominoes?"

"Just as you prefer," he said, grinning. "Do you fancy yourself as a Grecian goddess?"

She wrinkled her charming nose at him and turned impetuously to her sister.

"Liza, the most delightful thing! Tony has invited us to a masquerade at the Pantheon next Thursday. Are we free that evening, do you know?"

"We are promised to Lady Spencer for her daughter's ball, Dearest."

Carina's face lost its look of eager anticipation.

"Oh, dear, I had quite forgotten. Tony did you receive a card for Amelia Spencer's ball?"

"Yes, but I sent regrets. Why?"

"Well, I was wondering if we might look in on the masquerade for an hour or two, then go to Lady Spencer's. What do you say to that idea, Liza?"

Elizabeth seemed a trifle discomfited, but before she could speak the earl put in smoothly:

"I fear Sir Anthony has been a bit indiscreet, my dear Carina, in inviting such a young girl to the Pantheon. He forgets that the Pantheon masquerades draw a—shall we say *mixed* crowd? It really is no longer the place for young ladies of quality. You would not care for it."

Carina was aware that Tony had turned scarlet, and she felt anger leaping into being not only for the sake of his embarrassment at the earl's hands but because of the hateful look of superiority on the handsome face of her sister's escort. As usual she plunged into speech unwisely.

"It is good of you to be so concerned for our reputations, my lord, but since we should remain masked the entire time, surely the risk of creating talk is negligible?" Although she strove to remain cool, her words sounded almost rude even to her own ears. Nevertheless she continued to meet the earl's mocking glance squarely.

He said gently, "I think in this case you must allow older and wiser counsel to prevail, my dear child."

"I am afraid I can see no reason to accept your judgment as a criterion for my behavior, my lord," she replied stiffly, aware that his attitude had brought forth uncivil behavior from herself but unable to prevent the words.

"Oh, I would not presume to govern your conduct, Miss Carina. I was referring to your aunt."

Carina's cheeks flamed at the blatant lie. He was succeeding famously in putting her in the wrong. How she detested him!

Elizabeth intervened before she could further disgrace herself in her anger at the officious Earl. "Guy is right, you know, Dearest. Aunt Augusta would never allow us to attend a Pantheon masquerade. I am sorry, Sir Anthony," she said to the silent youth sitting beside Carina.

He mumbled a deprecating apology, and if Carina had not chanced to glance at the earl at that moment, it is most probable that she would have accepted defeat with as good grace as she could muster. But she did glance at him and surprised a look of such smiling enmity as caused her heart to stop for an instant before it hammered on, and her resolution stiffened instantly. The curtain was rising on the last act but at the moment the play's enchantment had evaporated for Carina. In the darkened theater she seized Tony's arm and whispered urgently:

"Tony, will you be so obliging as to escort me to the masquerade?"

"But your sister said your aunt will not permit it; besides you are promised for the evening."

"Never mind that. Will you take me if I can contrive a way?"

Tony looked miserable. "I do not think you should . . ." he began, only to be interrupted by the coldest tone he had ever heard from the friendly girl at his side.

"Very well, if you do not wish to be my escort, Tony, I shall simply have to make arrangements with someone else."

"No, don't do that. I'll take you, my pleasure," he mumbled in a goaded voice from which any expectation of pleasure had vanished. "But how is it to be contrived?"

"We dare not talk here. I'll meet you in the park tomorrow. Abby and I shall be there at eleven. Will that be convenient?"

He nodded and they both relapsed into silence although Carina's attention never did revert entirely to the drama on the stage so engrossed was she in planning a strategy to defeat the odious earl in something. However she summoned up all her own acting ability later to bid him a pleasant good night and thank him charmingly for the evening's pleasure.

Miss Silverdown, who had heard none of the pertinent discussion about the proposed masquerade, yawned delicately and went up to her bed-chamber after a few words with her nieces. Carina's instincts prompted escape from her sister's speculative eyes but she admirably controlled her urge to flee and chatted gaily of their evening as they made their way more slowly upstairs. When she paused briefly Elizabeth said regretfully:

"I hope you were not too disappointed to have to refuse Sir Anthony's invitation, Carina, but the Pantheon has become so much a haunt of the vulgar lately that it is no longer considered a suitable place for young girls. Guy was absolutely right, you know."

"Well, I was disappointed, of course, but it was the fact that you said Aunt would not permit it that changed my mind. Guy Accrington has no right to decide how I shall behave or where I shall go." Her chin went up and she looked frankly at her sister who said quickly:

"No, of course he has not, Dearest, but he did not wish you to go where you might be embarrassed. It was said for your own sake."

Carina maintained a silence, though in her firm opinion the earl had enjoyed embarrassing Tony and would derive a great deal of pleasure from seeing his prospective sister-in-law discomfited. In that one revealing look tonight she had been made to realize that her attempts to hide her dislike of him had not been convincing and that it was returned in full measure. However, there was no point in discussing the earl with Elizabeth. If she did not shrink from the thought of his being a fortune hunter, would she be influenced by his dislike of her sister? This was supposing Carina could even convince her of the earl's dislike which was questionable. He was a very plausible man and his attitude toward Carina was always one of affectionate tolerance. Well, she refused to think about the odious Earl any longer. She bade her sister good night and closed her own door, obtaining the privacy she needed to evolve a scheme for attending the masquerade.

The result of her cogitation was relayed to a somewhat reluctant Sir Anthony the following day when they met by appointment and walked together for a while in the park. To Abby's eyes the meeting was accidental and she dropped behind good-naturedly to allow them to talk privately. It was not unusual for one or the other sister to make quick trips abroad to accomplish some small errand and Abby was frequently recruited to accompany either on these occasions. This morning Carina had offered to pick up some ribbon for her sister when she exchanged books at Hookham's, and they had detoured by the park to admire the flowers. Now Carina explained earnestly to a dubious Sir Anthony:

"It really should not be at all difficult to achieve, Tony, if you write a note to Lady Spencer saying you find you will be able to attend Amelia's ball after all. At some point in the evening we shall simply slip out and drive to the Pantheon in your carriage—you do have a carriage at your disposal, have you not?"

He nodded. "I had planned to use m' mother's that evening, anyway."

"Excellent!" She beamed a smile at him. "We can slip out unobserved and return before the ball breaks up with no one being the wiser. There is really very little risk involved."

Sir Anthony frowned and bit his lower lip in indecision.

"It sounds simple enough," he admitted, "but it may not be so easy to reenter the Spencers' house unnoticed."

"Why not, if you bribe the porter not to announce us? Will he recognize you?"

"Oh, yes, I have dined there on several occasions. Jack Spencer is a friend of mine." He still looked far from happy, but Carina blithely went on:

"There is just one little thing, Tony. I can easily hide a silk half mask in my reticule but I do not think I can manage to smuggle a domino into our carriage without Liza or Aunt Augusta seeing it." She raised hopeful eyes to his. "Do you think you might procure one for me and hide it in your carriage? I will pay you for it."

He laughed and for the first time seemed to enter into the spirit of the adventure. "You are the complete intrigante. Do not worry about that aspect of the affair. M' mother is a little thing like you. I'll borrow one from her. She never throws anything away."

Carina smiled gaily up at him. "Thank you, Tony. I am greatly looking forward to this. We shall have a most diverting evening."

"Not too diverting, I hope. Edgemere was right in a way, you know. All kinds of people frequent the Pantheon. Oh, they won't trouble you when you are with me, but it will not be what you are used to." He quirked one eyebrow and searched her face with unsmiling brown eyes. "You may still cry off, you know."

"Never. It is high time I saw a little more of life than is permitted to young ladies of quality." She made a wry face. "Sometimes I feel girls like me are too well protected. We are scarcely aware of what goes on in the world around us. Well, I must go now. Thank you so much, Tony."

Carina was not quite so imperturbably decided as she hoped she had convinced Tony she was. In the days remaining she ran the gamut from utter determination to carry out her plan through silent uneasiness to an unhappy conviction that she would be betraying Liza and behaving in a thoroughly irresponsible if not actually scandalous manner. When she reached this point she jerked herself up again mentally. After all, what was so irretrievably wicked about wishing to see a little more of life than the glimpses allowed a typically overprotected debutante? As long as she remained masked she would avoid even the breath of scandal. What would she be doing, after all, except visiting for a brief time, and well escorted, a rather less genteel establishment than she was used to? Described in such terms it did seem paltry to suffer any qualms of courage or conscience. The only aspect of the situation her brain refused to consider was the importance to be ascribed to the earl's objections. She shied away from acknowledging even to herself how deeply she was motivated by a desire to defy successfully the detested Lord Edgemere in something. He was having things too much his own way lately. She could not bear to think of her beautiful sister throwing herself away on such an unworthy suitor. She would take the successful carrying out of her little adventure against his advice as a good omen for his eventual complete vanquishment.

After all her tortuous mental skirmishing, the actual escape was ludicrously easy to accomplish. Tony claimed her for a dance at the Spencer ball and they made their unobtrusive way to the exit without drawing any curious stares. Thanks to Tony's careful planning and a large *douceur*, the carriage arrived precisely as they left the house. Carina was wearing only a light gauze shawl over her gown, but the attractive blue silk domino provided by Tony was quickly donned in the carriage and she was too excited to feel cold in any case. She was grateful for his assistance in tying the strings of her black silk half mask, as her fingers were strangely awkward. When they entered the Pantheon shortly afterward, the masked man in the black domino and the slight figure in blue with a concealing hood drawn up to cover bright hair could not have been identified by the persons closest to them. Indeed they were more anonymous than many of the patrons who had already seen fit to discard their masks. Not all wore the concealing dominoes either. All sorts of historical and legendary characters were seen parading the spacious rooms or dancing to the music provided by an orchestra set up on a stage at one end of the large, rectangular ballroom. At first Carina was too entranced with the ornate decor to give more than a passing glance to the participants. She blinked at the splendor of huge crystal chandeliers ablaze in the main ballroom and the innumerable smaller ones suspended in each arch supported by gilded pillars around the periphery.

It might be considered incredibly vulgar by persons of taste, but one must concede that it was considerably more impressive than Almack's. Tony laughed at her bemused expression and swept her unceremoniously into a dance.

Even to Carina's inexperienced eyes there was a different atmosphere from the decorum that marked the Assemblies at Almack's. It seemed noisier for one thing, and the couples on the floor did not always content themselves with conversing with each other but hailed friends (at least Carina assumed the persons so jubilantly addressed must be friends) loudly and exchanged quips with other dancers. There was much more obvious merriment and Carina was dimly aware of accents that were never heard in genteel circles. She supposed innocently that the license allowed by anonymity was mainly responsible for the lack of restraint shown by several ladies who actually ogled the gentlemen and approached some with whom, judging by their reception, Carina could not suppose them to be at all acquainted. She was too fascinated in a faintly repellent sense to bear her fair share in conversation with her own escort, and for his part, Tony seemed to be finding it increasingly difficult to initiate conversation himself. She wondered if he regretted bringing her and was casting about in her mind for something to say that would assuage the sense of guilt she suspected he was harboring when a sharp jab on her ankle surprised a gasp of pain from her lips. The couple who had careened into her danced blithely away, but Tony stopped and looked at her with concern.

"Are you hurt?"

"No, no, it is of no consequence, but I fear my flounce has torn," she said ruefully, lifting her skirts for a closer inspection. "I have some pins in my reticule fortunately. There must be some place where I can effect a repair in privacy."

"Yes, of course. I'll ask someone."

Tony made inquiries and Carina retired presently, assuring him cheerfully that she would not be a moment.

CHAPTER 8

It lacked only thirty minutes to midnight when Mr. Gavin Delawney entered the well-lit, over-crowded rooms of the Spencers' spacious Berkeley Square mansion. Knowing Lady Spencer for one of the most inveterate of matchmaking mamas with two successes to her credit in two successive years, he had always been chary of accepting her numerous invitations. He would not have come tonight had he not expected to see the Raven sisters here. He speculated that it must have cost Lady Spencer a pang to have to present her pallid, sadly freckled Amelia in company with two of the loveliest girls in town, but she would not have it said she lacked the courage to invite the nieces of one of her oldest friends. One could count on Lady Spencer never putting a foot wrong socially. His sister Bella had said earlier in laughing warning to him that she must be part sorceress to have succeeded in turning off in rapid succession two girls with few pretensions to beauty, no claim to social brilliance and very modest portions, so he had best look sharp if her maternal eye should chance to fall on him. Gavin had laughed but had taken care not to be too readily available when Lady Spencer issued invitations. Tonight, however, he was in a reckless humor and dared to gratify his hostess by dancing with her third daughter, an insipid girl with little conversation. At least she danced gracefully, he thought resignedly as he returned the tongue-tied girl to her parent with a charming bow and a smile that sent unaccustomed color into Amelia's cheeks and a familiar gleam to her mother's eye.

His duty gracefully performed he felt free to seek amusement with girls more to his taste and scanned the rooms hoping for a glimpse of either of the Raven sisters. He did not see Carina, but after roaming through ballroom and supper room, he came unexpectedly upon Elizabeth as she was leaving a small saloon. He thought her appearance lacked something of her customary serenity and his conjecture was proved quite correct by her first words.

"Gavin, have you seen Carina this evening?" To his acute senses her casual tones held an undercurrent of anxiety.

"No, but I arrived a scant twenty minutes ago. Why?"

For a moment there was silence while he sensed the battle she was waging against herself, then she made a helpless little gesture with her hands. "I cannot find her," she admitted simply.

His eyes narrowed thoughtfully. "But you have your suspicions?" he suggested, watching her closely.

Elizabeth gave an annoyed little laugh. "Oh, yes," she sighed, "I have my suspicions. I think she is at the Pantheon masquerade."

Although he had few illusions about Carina, that caught him unawares. "What!" he questioned

sharply. "How? With whom? Have you told anyone else of your suspicions?"

"Tony Mercer invited us and I told him Aunt
would never permit it. I knew Carina was disappointed but I thought she had accepted it." She
hesitated momentarily and he raised an interrogat-
ing eyebrow. She continued more slowly in flattened accents: "Lord Edgemere was present at
the time and I think his obvious censure put up
Carina's back."

He snorted impatiently. "It would, of course.
The little idiot thrives on opposition."

Elizabeth prudently ignored this ungentlemanly assessment of her sister.

"Carina detests him. She has warned me that
he is a fortune hunter. He is here tonight but I
hesitated to ask his help in the circumstances."

"Quite rightly," he put in quickly, thankful for
this small blessing. "The fewer people who know
the better. What makes you think she has actually
gone there?"

"Tony had not planned to accept Lady Spencer's invitation but he was here earlier tonight
and danced with Carina. I have seen neither for
almost an hour."

Gavin noticed one of Elizabeth's swains approaching.

"Don't worry, I'll find her. Do not confide in
anyone else. I'll bring her back here if possible,
but if it grows too late I shall take her directly
home and you must set it about that she became
ill and left with Tony."

He bowed over Elizabeth's hand and sauntered
slowly toward the huge stairway, acknowledging
friends but allowing no one to detain him. Once

outside however, his indolent attitude dropped
from him like a peeled skin and he quickly hailed
a hackney and was on his way to Oxford Street
with no time wasted. Indeed there was none to
waste if he was to restore the wretched brat to her
sister before Miss Silverdown thought to leave the
Spencers'. He told himself he was scarcely surprised, having always known Carina would contrive to ruin herself by some irresponsible act.
During the uncomfortable ride in the decrepit
hackney, he consoled himself with the thought of
the pleasure he would derive from wringing Carina's beautiful neck, and Tony's too for abetting
her in the foolhardy scheme. Not that he attribut-
ed this little plot to Tony, rattle though he was.
He well knew who had masterminded the affair.
Unless she was completely harebrained she must
have planned to return to the Spencers'; perhaps
even now they were on their way back there and
he was embarked on a fool's errand. He almost
signaled the jarvey to turn around but decided to
go on on the off chance that the quarry was still
at the Pantheon. On arriving he was confronted
with the problem of a lack of either costume or
domino but solved that expeditiously by purchas-
ing at an outrageous price a black domino and
mask from a gentleman leaving the premises as he
arrived.

Once safely inside it soon became apparent that
the task of locating anybody amongst the highly
unidentifiable masses was no sinecure. The ballroom was crowded with domino-clad damsels.
Several were tiny like Carina, but after unsuccess-
fully stalking three of them for a glimpse of their
faces and finding it necessary himself to repulse

the persistent advances of a pair of unmasked beauties of Covent Garden notoriety, he beat a strategic retreat to the outer saloons to gather his forces. He was sweating by now and it was not entirely due to the oppressive heat of the place. The little idiot must have realized by now how unsuitable the atmosphere was. Damn Tony's eyes for bringing her here! Nothing was going to deprive him of the pleasure of planting him a facer.

He rounded a corner and came upon a couple standing close together in apparent argument. The slight figure in a blue domino was about Carina's size, but her hair was concealed by the hood and he caught only an unrevealing glimpse of cheek and jawline. Her escort was much too big to be Tony Mercer, however, and he was about to pass by when the man wrapped an arm around the girl's waist and kissed her forcibly. She had twisted her face so as to spoil his aim but one of her hands was pinned helplessly to her side by the encircling arm. Gavin had reluctantly decided to intervene when the victim balled her other hand into a small fist and struck her aggressor a vicious jab to his midsection, sending him reeling back momentarily. "Left-handed and below the belt," Gavin noted with perverse satisfaction. Evidently she had learned something at that mill, overrated or not. Having positively identified his prey from this unladylike action, he sprang forward before the enraged recipient of the blow had recovered enough from the shock to take punitive action.

"I'll teach you, you little . . ."

Even as Gavin thrust Carina unceremoniously

behind him, the man in the purple domino was reaching for her slim form with beefy red hands.

"Oh, no, you don't, my buck. If you think the lady did not make her objections to your advances quite clear, I'll be more than delighted to add my brand of persuasion to hers."

Carina had gasped at the sound of his voice and he smiled grimly. His opponent topped him by a couple of inches and outweighed him by at least three stone however, and he was not impressed.

"Get out of my way," he growled briefly. "No little flash-talking doxy is going to hit Jack Tanner and get away with it."

"This lady," said Gavin coolly, emphasizing the second word, "happens to be my wife and you'll deal with me first. Right here and now if you like."

"Your wife?" For a moment there was a throbbing silence fraught with danger as the visibly taken aback Jack Tanner considered the inadvisability of indulging his urgent need for physical reprisal. Carina clasped her trembling hands and lips tightly together to prevent any action on her part that might endanger Gavin any further. At last the big man said slowly, disappointment evident in his whole bearing,

"Well, I wish you joy of the little vixen. I hope you beat her regularly." He turned to the silent Carina and executed a mocking bow. "My compliments, ma'am," he sneered and, turning on his heel, strode away.

"I'd like to think your unfortunate husband would heed that very sound advice," Gavin said coldly, taking her firmly by the arm. "By the way, what have you done with Mercer?"

"I had to repair a torn flounce. Tony was supposed to wait for me here. How did you recognize me?" she demanded abruptly.

"I am acquainted with no other female capable of delivering a body blow," he stated, still in that cold, repressed tone.

Carina ignored this, having just digested the implication evident in his previous remarks. "How did you know I was here with Tony?" she gasped, feeling the initial warning of alarm for her own sake since she had first embarked on this adventure.

"Your sister told me. Is this Tony approaching?" He nodded toward a black-domino-clad figure coming rapidly toward them.

She made no answer, being totally involved in turning over his words in her mind.

"This lady is with me," the new black domino said firmly, taking her other arm. "You will excuse us, please."

"No, I won't," replied Gavin shortly. "I'm taking her back to the Spencers'. How did you get here?"

The other man started nervously but Carina said hastily:

"It's all right, Tony. This is Gavin Delawney. He rescued me from a surly brute. Where were you anyway?"

"Right where I said I'd be," he answered hotly. "You must have come out a different entrance."

Carina glanced around at her surroundings. "Oh, dear heaven, so I did. I am sorry, Tony, if I worried you."

"Are you equally disturbed over worrying your sister into a distracted state?" Gavin inquired nastily, then repeated his earlier question to Sir Anthony. "How did you get here?"

"I have my carriage. We planned to slip back into the Spencers' ball without anyone being the wiser."

"Then get it now. I'll stay with Carina. We'll give you ten minutes before going outside."

After Tony had left them with a worried glance at the suddenly pale girl (if the portion of her face uncovered by the black mask was a true indication), a long silence ensued between the remaining two persons in the corridor. Carina could not break it and seemingly Gavin would not. Perhaps he had spoken to her for the last time ever, Carina thought wildly as she stood there stubbornly erect but inwardly quaking before the anger and disgust she could feel emanating from her erstwhile good companion.

After a silent eternity Gavin inquired casually:

"Just what would you have done had I not appeared at that precise moment? I feel sure such a resourceful young lady must have had a plan to handle the situation."

The words of appreciation she had been preparing for his timely rescue froze on her lips as his polite sarcasm washed over her with the burning quality of lye.

"I'd have run, of course. I am a very fleet runner. It was your sudden appearance that prevented me." She returned his stare with well-feigned composure.

"Well, I must, of course, accept your own estimation of your speed, but in those hampering skirts?" he drawled, nodding at her domino and ruffled yellow gown. "I would imagine in your previous races you have probably been garbed as a boy."

The unerring accuracy of this shaft caused the blood to flame into Carina's cheeks, and she turned her back on him, furious that he had guessed she was used to racing with the village youths dressed in Robbie's clothes.

After this there was no more conversation until Gavin indicated it was time to go outside. The carriage was just pulling into place as they exited and Gavin allowed Tony to assist the silent girl into it. It was a lovely late spring night, warm and soft and well lit by a three-quarter moon of pale gold. This pleasant circumstance apparently went completely unnoticed by the silent trio in the carriage. Not until they came into Berkeley Square did any one of the occupants venture a comment, then Gavin offered to go on ahead so that he might warn them if their entrance looked like being remarked. As it turned out, their reentry went as smoothly as their unremarked exit two hours previously. Carina breathed a sigh of relief when she saw her sister in conversation with Gavin, but this rapidly evolved into a pang of regret as Gavin bowed over her sister's hand and strode away before Carina could reach them.

If Elizabeth noticed the wounded look her sister wore as she paused involuntarily and stared after his retreating form, she was tactful enough to refrain from questioning her at that moment. Beyond assuring herself that no harm had come to Carina, she did not mention the subject uppermost in both their minds until much later when, having seen her aunt safely off to bed, she knocked at her sister's door.

Carina bade her enter. She was sitting in the middle of the bed, very young and anxious as she nervously eyed her sister, still dressed in her white sarcenet ball gown, looking as crisp and fresh as she had five hours previously. As Elizabeth slowly approached the four-poster, however, Carina had to revise her initial impression. There was a tired droop to her sister's mouth and the beautiful blue eyes were vaguely worried. Any lingering rebelliousness dropped from Carina and she blurted hastily before Elizabeth could speak:

"I am sorry, Liza, truly I am, to have worried you."

Elizabeth silenced her with a raised hand.

"Why, Carina? Why did you do such a dangerous thing?"

Carina hung her head. She had expected this eminently reasonable question, of course, and yet she was not at all sure she could offer a reasonable explanation. At this point she was not at all positive she even knew why she had done what she had. The disturbing thought, gnawing like a worm, that she had been merely childishly defiant robbed her of all verbal initiative. The silence lengthened. She raised a troubled face to her sister.

"Dearest, did the fact that Guy Accrington was so opposed to the idea influence you at all?"

"I fear it must have been the deciding factor," Carina admitted ruefully, her innate honesty forcing the confession. "I know you like him, Liza"— she was frowning in concentration and failed to see her sister's instinctive gesture of denial—"and perhaps it is my abominable pride that has caused me to take him in such dislike, but I react to him like a cat to a strange dog. I . . . I bitterly resented his coming the stern parent over me and embarrassing Tony into the bargain. It seemed if I could only oppose him successfully in this it would be a good omen that his game would be queered on all suits." She raised her open hands palm up in a helpless gesture. "I do not think I *can* explain more logically, Liza; it was not really logical but an instinctive defiance."

Elizabeth's expression was completely serious and she spoke musingly as if to herself. "It will never do then. I had not fully understood how deeply you disliked him until tonight."

"What will never do?"

"Marriage to Guy, of course. Not that he has made me an offer yet but I fear he will soon. Naturally if you dislike the idea so much, I will refuse him."

Carina regarded her sister in astonishment tinged with dismay. "Liza, you cannot decide a question as important as marriage because your little sister has taken the man in dislike."

Elizabeth's chuckle was genuinely amused. "Do not look so aghast, Dearest. If I thought for a time of accepting Guy, it was because, as I told you once, I had grown weary of being the much-sought-after Raven heiress. Since I must marry sometime it seemed a possible solution. I realize now I was merely suffering from a fit of the dismals at the time. Guy and I would not suit. It will be much better to wait awhile."

"Liza, it would be better to wait forever than to marry for such a reason."

Elizabeth stared unseeingly into her sister's desperately earnest eyes. For a fleeting second Carina was struck by some quality of hopelessness in her sister's expression, then the bronze lashes flickered down to conceal her thoughts as she said lightly,

"I am persuaded you are quite right, Dearest. Now tell me what happened tonight. What was the Pantheon like?"

"Oh, most impressive if decidedly ostentatious—all gilded pillars and crystal chandeliers." She wrinkled her nose adorably. "I must admit Lord Edgemere was quite correct about the type of persons who attend Pantheon balls, however. Very loud and vulgar. You would not credit the pushing manner of some of the women there. They positively ogle the gentlemen, just begging for their attentions. I assure you I blushed for my sex. It was very diverting at first, but we never intended to remain above a half hour or so. We thought to be back before anyone missed us from the Spencers'. I never meant you to be worried, Liza."

"I am sure you did not, Carina, but it was a risky thing to do all the same. I am quite out of charity with Tony Mercer and so I shall tell him when next we meet."

"No, pray do not, Liza. All the blame was mine. I persuaded Tony against his will; indeed, I told him if he would not take me I would make arrangements to go with someone else."

"Poor Tony. That was nothing less than moral blackmail." Elizabeth tried to look stern, but there was the faintest trembling about her lips and she did not quite meet her sister's eyes. However, Carina was wallowing in self-blame at this point and she needed no additional reproaches. She hesitated a moment then proceeded with a little difficulty, keeping her eyes on her linked fingers.

"I fear Gavin is very angry. He knows the whole scheme was my fault—in fact he told me so—but I greatly fear he means to give Tony a most undeserved tongue-lashing at the very least. He is quite brutal," she finished, raising a slightly flushed face dominated by gray eyes darkened with resentment.

Elizabeth's delicate brows arched in surprise.

"How is this? Did anything occur that you have not thought fit to mention as yet? You may as well tell me the whole," she added as Carina hesitated, "if you do not wish me to ask Tony or Gavin."

"Tony doesn't know—at least he did not see the incident. Everything would have gone smoothly and we would have left before Gavin arrived had not a clumsy oaf trod on my gown, tearing the flounce. I had to retire to pin it, and when I finished somehow I mistook the entrance where Tony was waiting and came out another door. There was a big brute there and he grabbed me and kissed me." At Elizabeth's horrified exclamation she said with savage satisfaction: "Never mind, I punched him in the stomach and would easily have evaded him had not Gavin chosen that moment to appear." Her voice shook with resentment. "Naturally he witnessed the incident and came wading in in that detestably cool manner of his to threaten the man if he did not leave at once, which he was not at all inclined to do, let me tell you, being taller and much heavier than Gavin. For an instant I was in a panic that they would come to blows, but Gavin told him I was his wife and that stopped him from tearing in, though it went much against the grain with him to forgo punishing me for repulsing him. He told Gavin he hoped he beat me regularly and," she finished with a burst of fury, "Gavin said later he hoped my husband would heed that excellent advice. My *unfortunate* husband, to be exact. He is the most detestable man I know."

Elizabeth smiled and said slyly, "More so than Lord Edgemere?"

"They are equally detestable," Carina affirmed stubbornly.

"Gavin mentioned none of this to me. Small wonder he is annoyed, my dear. I have more to thank him for than I thought."

"He is an officious, interfering busybody—and a brute into the bargain!"

"To whom I am deeply indebted and so should you be," said Elizabeth sternly. "Now off to sleep with you. You have had a most adventurous evening. I am persuaded no one missed you at the ball. Aunt was in the card room all evening, and there was such a crush in the ballroom and drawing rooms I feel sure your absence went unremarked."

Carina strove for a casual tone. "Did Edgemere know?"

"No, I did not confide my suspicions to him."

"Thank heavens for that," Carina said fervently.

"As you say. Now to sleep, Dearest."

CHAPTER 9

Nearly a week later Carina was shopping in Bond Street with Abby when a sporty phaeton expertly driven by a man in a multicaped driving coat pulled up just ahead. Carina's heart gave a little leap of delight at the sight of that familiar dark red head. She had tried not to think of Gavin during the past week because of an unfamiliar feeling of desolation induced by the fear that he might have written her off as a vulgar hoyden. Now, however, at sight of his casual smile and careless, "Hop in, brat. Tell your maid I'll bring you safe home," she experienced a perverse stab of irritation that he should act as though they had parted only yesterday on the best of terms. Perhaps it had slipped his mind that he had been abominably rude to her at their last meeting and had actually stalked away from her so as not to have to speak to one for whom he felt nothing save disgust, but the scene was still sharp in her memory. She noted that Finkston was not in his usual place and turned rainwater-clear eyes in an unsmiling face to his.

"You wish me to drive with you without even the vestige of a chaperone?" she inquired coolly.

A mocking gleam lit his own eyes. "You must

forgive me if the thought did not occur that you would regard that circumstance as an impediment to social intercourse, unless, of course, Tony was carrying a concealed chaperone on a recent occasion that leaps to mind."

By a strong effort of will Carina prevented a blush from rising, but her hands in blue kid gloves clenched into fists briefly before she brought under control her resentment of the taunt. The movement did not escape his notice and the amusement in his eyes deepened.

"You may deliver yourself of your opinion of my manners and conduct much more effectively in privacy. Will you come? My horses are fresh and I cannot keep them standing indefinitely."

Indeed the highly bred grays were already on the fret at the enforced wait. Carina transferred her packages to Abby's willing hands and climbed lightly up into the high-perch phaeton, disdaining the hand he offered to assist her ascent. His attention was entirely taken up by the mettlesome pair for the next few moments as he eased them out into the stream of traffic, and Carina was forced to grudging admiration of his skill at handling them in the bustling city traffic as they approached Piccadilly. Her irritation was already melting away in the pleasure of driving in an open carriage on a lovely day.

Presently he slanted a glance at her.

"Well, brat, have you come down from your high ropes or did you accept my invitation merely to deliver a lecture about my ungentlemanly treatment of you at our last unfortunate meeting?"

This provocative remark aroused only mild annoyance in one who found grudge bearing heavy work at best. "You behaved abominably," she said without heat, staring straight ahead.

"Yes, I fear I did."

His reply startled her in its unexpectedness and she turned questioning eyes to his serious face.

"You see, I am inclined to forget how young you are and I was worried that your little adventure might have serious consequences. Am I forgiven?" He turned his head and smiled at the flowerlike face regarding him, and this time a betraying flush crept up over her creamy skin, lending a sparkle to the clear eyes. He continued to stare at her for some few seconds, a deep question in his own eyes.

Carina's gaze faltered and she averted her face slightly, overcome by something she could not explain, for never before in her life had she experienced shyness. As from afar she heard his soft chuckle and searched wildly for words with which to ease the tension.

"I . . . I am not so very young, you know. My eighteenth birthday was last week," she stammered inanely.

"Was it really? How remiss of me to ignore such an important event. I must remedy that omission promptly." The familiar bantering note was in his voice and Carina relaxed perceptibly. Here was the Gavin she knew and trusted. For a palpitating interval she had been confronted with a stranger whose magnetic eyes seemed to affect her breathing strangely.

"I would like you to meet someone," he said abruptly. "That is why I wished to take you up."

"Oh, who?"

"My sister. I caught a glimpse of her new turnout entering the park a few minutes ago. I rather think you will take to each other. Bella was a madcap too, before she was married. Still is for that matter, but now that she is increasing Melton keeps a firmer check on her."

They had neared Hyde Park corner now and he proceeded to enter by the gate near Apsley House. The carriage road was crowded with vehicles of all descriptions on such a glorious day. They had driven nearly all the way around before Gavin located his sister's smart standard phaeton upholstered in coffee-colored leather. It was halted while Lady Melton chatted amiably with two dowagers in a barouche, but as Gavin pulled a little way ahead, she brought her conversation to an end and the barouche moved off, one of its dignified occupants bowing formally to Gavin while the other raked Carina with an assessing though not unkind eye.

Gavin turned to Carina with a mischievous grin.

"Are you up to holding the reins while I bring Bella over here?"

"Naturally," that intrepid young lady replied without a qualm, not deeming it at all necessary to mention that, while she had often tooled the gig around Ravenshill, none of her pleas to her father had moved him from his reluctance to teach her to drive a pair.

"They should be all right, now I've worked the fidgets out of them," Gavin promised soothingly, and walked briskly back to his sister's carriage from which he presently assisted her to descend, leaving the groom to hold the horses.

In a moment he had returned with Lady Melton and handed her up into his own place while effecting a brief introduction. As he took the reins from Carina's slackened grasp, the two ladies shook hands, studying each other with identical candid expressions, both apparently approving what they saw. Lady Melton's blue eyes, so like her brother's, appraised the vibrant, unaffected girl beside her, liking the friendly gray eyes and short curls revealed by a fetching bonnet of chip straw that tied rather dashingly under one ear with a broad blue ribbon that matched Carina's kid gloves and half boots. Her smart walking dress of blue and cream flattered the petite perfection of her figure. In her turn, Carina was captivated by the delicate prettiness of this girl with the light brown curls and lovely pink and white complexion. She may have been dressed in the height of fashion in an emerald green carriage dress and matching hat, but to Carina's amazed eyes she appeared too young to be married and it was impossible to accept her as a prospective mother even though she was aware that Lady Melton was actually some two years older than Elizabeth.

She was regretting now in a light sweet voice that when she had heard so much about the Ravens from her brother, her curtailed social schedule had prevented her from meeting Miss Raven until this moment. She cast a mischievous look at her brother that subtracted another year or two from her age and caused Carina to stiffen slightly as she wondered just what Gavin may have disclosed of his knowledge of herself. At her slanted glance from under her lashes, he laughed and said in provokingly smooth tones:

"How can you doubt that it was everything of

the most complimentary?" She was not at all sure she appreciated Gavin's ability to guess her thoughts, but his sister was adding to her statement that Gavin had called Carina quite the best horsewoman of his acquaintance.

"I wish that we might ride together sometime, but unfortunately my doctor has curtailed my riding until after the baby is born. You did know . . .?" she broke off in slight confusion.

"Yes, Gavin has told me. I felicitate you most sincerely. You must. be thrilled." Carina's smile was warm and brought a tender glow to the other girl's eyes.

"Oh, yes. We have been married for almost three years, you see, and had begun to fear—but enough about me. This is your first season, I understand. Are you enjoying it?"

"Very much indeed, although there are times, especially on a day such as this, when I miss the country quite desperately."

"I shall be going down to the country in a few days now." She turned to her brother who was patiently standing by the horses and said reproachfully, "It was too bad of you to delay presenting me to Miss Raven until so late in the season, Gavin. We are removing to Melton on Friday. The doctor feels I shall benefit from the country air though I declare I could not feel better now that I am over the vaporish stage."

Carina said hesitantly, "If you are not too rushed with preparations to leave, I would very much like you to meet my sister and aunt. Perhaps Gavin might bring you to call one afternoon before your departure."

"How kind of you. I could come tomorrow if

Gavin finds this convenient." On being assured of
his willingness to escort her to Green Street, Lady
Melton went on to say she fancied she had seen
Miss Elizabeth Raven on one or two occasions the
previous year but had not had the pleasure of
making her acquaintance. "Your sister is a blonde,
is she not, and quite ravishingly beautiful?"

"To spare Carina's blushes I shall assure you
that your assumption is quite correct, Bella. Elizabeth is one of the loveliest girls in London. Good
looks run in the family as you can see," he finished, pointedly staring at Carina.

Lady Melton's laugh tinkled into the silence
caused by Carina's suddenly tongue-tied state.
"For shame, Gavin, to say you would spare Miss
Raven, then to proceed to embarrass her, and
with such *obvious* gallantry too. I vow it is only
her good manners that prevent her from calling
you a flirt to your face."

"My technique must be rusting or I am getting
old," he admitted with false humility and a mocking gleam, enjoying Carina's flaming cheeks and
sparkling eyes. "I think before Carina's good manners and my horses' patience are exhausted that I
should return you to your carriage, Bella."

On his return Gavin merely raised his brows
and said, "Well?" as he took the reins and gave
his horses a flick with the whip.

Correctly interpreting this as a query about her
reaction to his sister, Carina said warmly, "Lady
Melton is a delightful person, but do you know,
Gavin, it is difficult to think of her as a married
woman—she looks so very young."

He said with mild surprise, "I never thought
about it, but you are quite correct. She looks no

older than you." Something in this seemed to give him pause, for he maintained a thoughtful silence for a time after sending one searching glance toward his companion. For her part, Carina was quite content to sit idly enjoying the passing scene.

"Are you in a particular hurry? Will you wait while I execute one brief commission?" Gavin asked presently as the phaeton exited onto Oxford street.

"Of course. It is a shame to rush home on such a day."

They were heading back toward Bond Street but found it impossible to enter because of an accident. Evidently a curricle had overturned an ancient carrier's cart, spilling a load of cane chairs into the street. The drivers of the respective vehicles had collected quite a crowd to witness their violent exchange of courtesies while the cart was reloaded. Gavin detoured past, planning to enter from one of the small streets leading into Bond. The narrow street was virtually deserted except for three boys scuffling on the left side. Carina glanced at them casually then placed an urgent hard on Gavin's arm.

"Oh, stop, please!"

Assuming she had dropped something he pulled up obediently. Carina was already descending, far less gracefully than usual.

"One of those boys is hurt," she said over her shoulder.

Alarmed, Gavin looked around for someone to hold the horses. The boys who had been fighting had run away but another urchin appeared from a doorway. "Here, hold them, boy," he ordered shortly and hurried back to where Carina was kneeling beside an unconscious boy of nine or ten years. She did not look up from her fingers which were folding a handkerchief into a pad.

"It is his head. There is a deep cut in the back that is bleeding dreadfully. Do you have a handkerchief I can use to tie mine firmly in place?"

"Of course." He offered his and bent to hold the inadequate square in place while she quickly tied his large handkerchief around the child's head.

She smiled at him gratefully but said anxiously, "He is so very pale; the shock, no doubt. This should be stitched. Which hospital is closest, St. George's?"

He frowned. "We cannot simply remove him. Hey, boy, do you know this lad?" he called to the boy by the horses.

"Naw, he don't live near here," came the unhelpful reply.

"Well," said Carina firmly, "we cannot leave him, and that cut needs attention—the pad is soaked already. If you will be so good as to hand him up to me, we can take him to the hospital."

She was climbing back into the phaeton while Gavin bent over and scooped up the still unconscious boy. He hesitated before placing him in Carina's outstretched arms. "You cannot take him, he's covered with blood."

"Nonsense, it is of no consequence. My gown is already dirty, from kneeling on the flagway. He must be supported."

Her calm, determined face and brisk tone reminded him of that other time on Hounslow Heath when she had coolly taken over the care of Miss Silverdown. He was amused at the faint hint of impatience in her manner and reluctantly complied with her request. After tossing a shilling to the boy lovingly and impartially stroking the horses, he gathered up the reins with twitching lips. "I think he'd have paid for the privilege of holding them. He hasn't even looked at the coin yet."

Carina smiled briefly, but her attention was taken up by the wretched scrap of humanity in her arms. Gavin's eyes lingered on the compassionate curve of her beautifully shaped mouth and he was almost overwhelmed by an urgent desire to press his own mouth to hers. Shaken by the strength of his wayward impulse, he tightened his hands on the reins, jerking the sensitive animals slightly.

Carina looked up and he essayed a stiff smile meant to reassure her. A moment later she said softly,

"Thank heavens he is coming around now," as her light burden stirred and groaned. "Don't be frightened," she said soothingly as fear flashed into the light blue eyes looking dazedly up at her. "You have cut your head, but we shall soon fix you up capitally. What is your name?"

His voice was little more than a hoarse croak. "Jeb Scott, ma'am."

"Well, Jeb, you will soon be feeling much more the thing."

To her distress two big tears squeezed out from under the boy's closed eyelids with their thick, stubby, almost white lashes and rolled down the thin cheeks, leaving twin clean, wet paths.

"Does it still hurt, Jeb?" she inquired tenderly,

shifting his slight body to a more comfortable position.

"It's not me 'ead, ma'am. Them dirty varmints took me money. I 'ad four shillings. I was going to buy some mutton for me mum." The tears were coming faster now and he gave a little hiccuping sob.

"Do not cry, Jeb, you shall have your four shillings back." She shot a glance at Gavin who nodded and said cheerfully,

"After we get your head fixed up we'll do your shopping for your mother and I'll take you home. Where do you live?" Jeb's reply meant nothing to Carina, but Gavin's lips tightened and he said firmly,

"I'll leave him in hospital to get fixed up while I take you home, then I'll get him and restore him to his 'mum.'"

"Oh, no, that is nonsensical. I do not mind waiting," Carina protested, but Gavin was adamant.

"You'll do as you are told for once."

She subsided into offended silence, but truth to tell, her arms were aching from the accumulated strain of bearing even so slight a burden as young Jeb. She held the horses while Gavin carried the now thoroughly frightened child into the forbidding brick structure that was St. George's Hospital.

He cast a pitiful look at Carina who smiled reassuringly at him.

"I know you are a brave boy, Jeb. Mr. Delawney will drive you home in this handsome carriage and you shall be able to sit up here where all your friends may see you." At this promise of heaven the boy's pale little face lit up like a candle and he managed a shy valedictory smile for Carina from Gavin's arms.

When the latter returned to retrieve his charge after leaving Carina at Green Street, he almost failed to recognize the pathetic scrap of humanity he had left less than an hour before. Grubby and bloodstained, tattered and terrified as he had been, Jeb could scarcely have been considered an appealing child, but now as he gazed back at Gavin a trifle shyly but with a jaunty air that was almost touching, Gavin could not prevent a sympathetic grin from appearing. The boy's answering smile revealed unexpectedly fine teeth, which, combined with large blue eyes, gave the pale little face a distinct attractiveness. Although the shabby garments were still bloodstained, his face and hands were clean and the flaxen hair was neatly brushed. The professional bandage that replaced Carina's effort gave him a slightly raffish air, and he came along with Gavin most trustingly until they got close enough to the phaeton to enable him to see Carina was not there.

"Where's the lady?" he demanded, stopping short and fixing Gavin with a vaguely accusing eye.

"I took her home, which I now propose to do for you. Up you get. Your mother will be worrying about you." He flipped a coin to the loafer holding the horses and climbed up after Jeb.

"The lady said as how I should 'ave my four shillings." His eyes now were distinctly worried.

"So you shall, and we'll stop at the market and buy that mutton too. Now you stop worrying and enjoy the ride."

This fine piece of advice was immediately acted upon by Jeb whose small face was glowing with pleasure when at last they drew up before a house in one of the dark, noisome alleys running off Farringdon Street. Within seconds a score of urchins had gathered round the phaeton, torn between admiration for the grays and bitter envy that Jeb should be so privileged as to be actually riding in such a bang-up job. They set up a clamor to be allowed to watch the horses. Gavin gave this office to one of the bigger boys with the devout hope that he would be able to protect the grays from unwanted attentions.

As a proud Jeb led the way up the steepest steps he had ever envisioned, Gavin carried in a box of provisions to the boy's amazed mother. When she saw the huge ham and packets of tea crowded into the box, tears came into her eyes and she murmured inarticulate thanks over and over again.

Gavin had been resolute in refusing to take Carina into a neighborhood that was only one degree removed from a back slum, but the woman was neatly dressed and the one room he saw, though sparsely furnished, was certainly clean. Two wide-eyed, blond little girls, younger than Jeb, eyed him timidly from a bed in a corner, but uttered no sound at all. He learned that Jeb's mother, still pretty though too thin and aged beyond her actual years, was a widow and struggled to support her family by working as a seamstress. Jeb made a very real contribution to the small family's precarious income by working for various shopkeepers in the West End.

Gavin was suffering acute embarrassment at the

fervency of the grateful mother's stammered thanks after Jeb told her the whole story of his afternoon's adventures, rendering the assault on his person unimportant except in that it led directly to the ecstatic experience of driving up to his house in full view of his natural enemies behind two beautiful prads in the slickest turnout ever invented. As Gavin prepared to take a somewhat awkward leave of the Scotts, Jeb came forward and stuck out his small hand.

"Tell the lady thankee for patching me 'ead. I liked 'er; she was pretty like me mum and she smelt nice. Someday I'm agoing to buy me mum something what smells like that."

"I'm quite sure you shall, Jeb," Gavin said, shaking hands with a manner as serious as the boy's, then he strode off to rescue his horses from the overeager attentions of a covey of children, scattering largesse as he went.

It was an extremely thoughtful young man who drove absently off. Part of his income derived from London properties. Until now he had never even bothered to discover their precise locations, let alone check on the condition of the buildings. Today's adventure had imbued him with a determination to effect a change in this state of affairs in the immediate future. His squirreling thoughts went from Mrs. Scott, valiantly striving to hold together her family under perilous conditions, to young Jeb with responsibilities beyond his age and capabilities, to Carina, who seemed so young and pampered, yet frequently surprised him by acting with a cool steadiness of purpose that belied her seemingly mercurial nature. He kept discovering new facets to Carina's character, not all of them pleasant surprises to be sure, but he had to admit she was an intriguing little witch. Today, for example, she had revealed a hitherto unsuspected compassion and a decidedly sweet maternal streak. In fact, a vision of Carina's face as she had looked while cradling the injured boy in her arms kept him company for the rest of the drive to the stable in the mews and the short walk around to his house.

CHAPTER 10

Carina was possessed of a great impatience to see Gavin the following afternoon. She looked forward to presenting his sister to Elizabeth and her aunt, of course, but her primary concern was to discover how her injured protégé had fared. She had managed to swallow her resentment yesterday at being returned like an unwanted parcel before the outcome had been learned, but she did think it unkind in Gavin not to have sent round a note at least to inform her of Jeb's condition. Consequently, she scarcely waited a polite interval after Lady Melton had been presented to Elizabeth and Miss Silverdown before drawing Gavin a little way apart and pouncing on him impatiently.

"Well, how did it come out?"

He surveyed the eager girl with indolent pleasure.

"Now how shall I answer that very ambiguous remark, I wonder?"

"Gavin, do not be a horrid tease. You know I desire to learn how Jeb Scott is. Did you take him home?"

"I am not at all certain I wish to relay information concerning another man for whom you appear to cherish a warm affection, especially when that feeling is strongly reciprocated." His teasing little smile widened. "Jeb says you are pretty and smell nice, thus aptly demonstrating that he is a lad of superior discernment. He also means to buy his mum perfume so she can smell like you."

Carina's dimples were in full play as she laughed delightedly. "Oh, how sweet of him. I trust he suffered no aftereffects of that fall?"

Gavin was forced to accept that it was well-nigh impossible to engage Carina in an agreeable flirtation. Was she more amenable to the advances of other men? he wondered suddenly. Tony Mercer, for instance? He overcame his sudden pique at this intrusive idea to reply with seeming casualness:

"Oh, no, he was in high gig to be able to dazzle his cronies on the street with his appearance in the phaeton."

Carina's smile had vanished. "Gavin, was it a very poor neighborhood?"

His hesitation was barely perceptible. "Not the worst, and his apartment was clean at least. The mother is a widow and I venture to say life is a struggle, but they seemed happy enough. There are two little girls also."

"Did you replace his four shillings? He was so worried."

He nodded. "We did some shopping for provisions. I felt you would wish that. The mother was pathetically grateful." He looked uncomfortable.

She smiled mistily at him. "Well, so am I pathetically grateful. Thank you, Gavin. I wonder if there is some way I may help him obtain some scent for his mother." She lapsed into a thoughtful silence which was disturbed by Elizabeth asking a question of Gavin. The conversation became general and remained so for the duration of Lady Melton's call.

Afterward it was apparent that her sister and aunt had been very favorably impressed with the lively Lady Melton, causing Carina to experience a small glow of pleasure that she was quite at a loss to explain.

But if the ladies enjoyed the visit of Lady Melton, the same could not be said of a very different type of visitation sustained by Elizabeth two days later. Ever afterward, Carina was to bless the impulse that caused her to bounce gaily in on her sister with some new purchases to display. She knew with absolute, bone-chilling certainty that Elizabeth would never have confided the reason for her obvious distress; indeed such was her self-discipline that she would have contrived to conceal her feelings from everyone had she been allowed an hour of privacy in which to recover her spirits. Thankfully, Carina's impulsive entrance hard upon her light tap on the door prevented this.

"Wait till you see what I found at . . ." She stopped abruptly, staring at the girl who sat up on the bed, quickly averting her face, but not before Carina noticed her flushed cheeks and wet lashes. "Liza, what's amiss? Are you ill?"

"No, no, that is nothing to signify. I have the headache a trifle, that is all." She wiped the back of her hand across her eyes in a half-furtive little gesture, all the while avoiding her sister's concerned glance.

Carina advanced slowly into the room, absently setting down her parcels on the dressing table. Her eyes never left her sister's face as she drew her yellow gloves off with meticulous care. "Somehow I do not think so," she said slowly. "You appear flushed rather than pale. What happened, Liza?"

"Nothing, Dearest. Already I am feeling better for my rest. What is it you have to show me?" Her determined attempt to achieve her usual calm demeanor twisted Carina's tender heart.

She sat down on the bed as Elizabeth made to rise and put her arm around her sister's shoulders, restraining her. "Please, Liza, do not try to bear it alone. Tell me what has happened to upset you."

Long-standing habits die hard. For years Elizabeth had protected and cared for her younger sister, listening to her problems, shielding her from her father's indifference and providing a constant emotional support. Her instinct was to shield Carina yet, but as she sat very still within the circle of her sister's strong young arm, something in the steady gray gaze from those tender eyes foretold a change in their relationship. Carina had definitely grown up and would henceforth meet her sister on more equal terms. She sighed slightly, unknowingly for herself, for it had been very satisfying to be needed.

"Please, Liza, let me help you. Shall I ring for tea up here?"

"Yes, that would be nice. Aunt is laid down with a touch of indigestion. She will not be expecting us."

They said very little until Abby had brought in the tea tray with alacrity and departed rather slowly. Something was up. According to Coleman Miss Elizabeth had emerged from the yellow saloon earlier, looking upset, and had issued orders that she was not at home to visitors. Now here was Miss Carina wearing an unusually serious face, and there were the packages they had carried home so gaily, still all wrapped on the table. She closed the door behind her with extreme reluctance.

Carina prepared her sister's tea and brought it to her where she sat gazing into the empty fireplace. "Now tell me what has occurred," she encouraged.

"Lord Edgemere called this afternoon. Coleman was not aware that Aunt had gone to lie down so I was alone when he arrived. I could scarcely refuse to admit him at that point although I was very formal, barely civil in fact." She sighed impatiently. "That had no apparent effect on him at all."

"Did he offer for you?"

Elizabeth nodded.

Carina's eyes narrowed and her lashes concealed her expression. "You were not so disturbed at having to refuse any of the others. Do you love him, Liza?"

"No! In fact I think I hate him!"

Carina blinked at this vehemence from the gentle Elizabeth, but she said nothing and her sister rushed on: "At first he simply ignored my refusal. He intimated that I was being coy or ... or *missish*. He ... he acted *indulgent*, as though he accepted that my odious popularity gave me the right to play-act in such a way, as though I should!" Her lovely white teeth fairly gnashed with remembered fury and Carina could not forbear to smile at her indignation. Elizabeth did not pause in her recital. "When I had succeeded in convincing him that I was not merely reciting lines from some dreadful play about a society Incomparable, but meant my refusal, he changed his approach again. He apologized for speaking too soon and assured me he would not press me for an immediate answer. He went on to say what a suitable match it would be in all respects, how our interests were the same, our tastes— Carina, it was like trying to talk to a foreigner who claimed to be able to speak English because he could say 'good morning' and 'how do you do?' My words did not penetrate his understanding."

"His conceit, rather," Carina put in dryly.

Elizabeth, who had laid her half-full cup on a small table and began a restless pacing, stopped and swung around to face her sister.

"I fear you are quite correct." Now her indignation was replaced by uneasiness. "He attempted to look brokenhearted and swore he loved me, which I do not credit for a moment. He promised he could make my affections animate toward him in time." She stopped suddenly and hot color suffused her pale cheeks.

Carina eyed her shrewdly. "I suppose he tried to make love to you?"

"How did you guess? He grabbed me quite roughly before I realized his intention and he ... he kissed me."

"Did you like it?"

"Carina!" Elizabeth's reproachful eyes met her sister's dancing gray ones. "Of course I did not like it, although I daresay he is quite an expert, having had so much experience."

"Did you tell him that?" Carina was serious now.

"I fear at that point I lost my temper and told him some few things I now greatly regret."

"Why regret?" Carina eyed her sister with new respect. "I did not know you even possessed a temper. You are always so cool and calm and ... and unstampedable."

Elizabeth laughed ruefully. "I wish I had not possessed a temper this afternoon. The earl is a proud man and, I fear, a dangerous one to cross."

"Oh, pooh, what can he do? Whatever did you say to him that you now regret?"

"Well I ... I told him he was no gentleman."

"Surely you do not regret that?" Carina continued to probe delicately.

"No, I ... I guess not." Elizabeth lapsed into silence.

"Well?"

Suddenly the words gushed out. "I told him there was absolutely no chance that my affections would ever animate toward him because they were already engaged elsewhere."

"Good for you. Did that stop him?"

"For the moment. He looked absolutely murderous and asked me if I was in the expectation of becoming betrothed in the immediate future." She stopped, her voice trailing off, looking completely miserable.

"I trust you told him it was none of his affair."

"No," Elizabeth whispered forlornly. "I told him the truth—that I had no such expectation, and then I left the room, left the earl just standing there and went to find Coleman to show him out. I simply could not bear any more of him at that moment." She took a deep, steadying breath and reseated herself, picking up the now cold cup and placing it to her lips.

Carina studied her sister drinking cold tea with no idea of what she was doing while rockets went off in her own head. Her calm, cool sister was in love, she must be, but with whom? Who amongst her acquaintance was so unattainable that she could sit there in frozen misery and hopelessness? No one surely. Feeling mean to probe Elizabeth's unhappiness but convinced of the necessity, she said gently,

"Was it also the truth that your affections are already engaged?"

At first Carina was afraid Elizabeth would shut her out as in the past, but after a short pause, while she painfully retained her breath, her sister whispered, "Yes."

"And does he not return your affection?"

"Once, a long time ago, I thought, I hoped he was not indifferent to me, but after all this time I must accept that he is just that—indifferent."

"All this time?" said Carina, startled. "Liza, how long have you loved this man?" Her brain reeled as her sister's whisper penetrated her consciousness.

"All my life, I think."

"Liza, is it Edward?"

"Yes, of course."

"But don't you know that he still loves you? He told me just a short time ago that that is why he avoids us, because he cannot bear to see you, knowing that *you* don't love *him*."

Elizabeth fastened onto the one important point.

"*Still* loves me? Edward *told* you he loves me?"

She jumped up from the chair. Her imploring eyes were filled with unshed tears and Carina felt her own misting as she hugged her sister fiercely.

"You silly goose, of course he still loves you. Only after Papa refused to let him pay his addresses to you, he felt— Liza!" Carina supported her suddenly sagging sister back into the chair and pushed her head down to her knees until the color returned to her face."

"You did not know." It was not a question. "Papa never even told you Edward wished to marry you. Oh, how could he do such a thing?"

Elizabeth looked at her out of eyes dulled with pain. "And all this time Edward has thought I knew, that I did not care. I . . . we could have been married long since. Oh, I must see him. I must explain." Her face was now glowing with anticipation. She would have risen from the chair but for Carina's restraining hands. She looked questioningly at her sister who said reluctantly,

"You could not have been married, you know, Liza. Papa refused Edward and would presumably still refuse him." Carina had suddenly recalled her father's sharp question on the night of her dance as to the frequency of Edward's visits.

Her very proper sister had surprised Carina more than once in the last half hour but never more so than by the resolute look she now directed at her from those beautiful blue eyes. Determination was written staggeringly clearly on the lovely face.

"In less than five months I shall come of age. Papa will have nothing to say to what I do then." Her words were quiet and quite unemotional. They were also completely devoid of any sem-

blance of filial obligation. Carina knew her sister
had strength enough to endure any trials which
beset her; witness how she had carried on smilingly for years while her heart yearned for Edward's love. Before today's revealing conversation
she would, however, have judged her to be one
of those females who would always sacrifice themselves on the altars of family duty and considerations of proper conduct for well-brought-up young
women. In truth she was rather awed by Elizabeth's cool determination to seek out the man she
wanted, now that she knew he felt the same way.

She was repeating, "I must see Edward immediately and explain."

"But you cannot simply approach a man and
tell him you love him," Carina protested feebly.

Elizabeth laughed merrily. "Can I not? You
know, Carina," she tilted her head on one side
and regarded her sister with mischievous eyes, "I
do believe, of the two Raven sisters, *you* are the
missish one." She laughed again at Carina's astounded expression, then said gently,

"Edward has waited for a long time and he is
too much of a gentleman to approach me under
the circumstances. If my love is worth anything it
will not wait upon pride. Were you going to offer
to act as a go-between for us?"

"Well, I . . . I suppose I was going to suggest
something of the sort."

"Thank you, Dearest, but I feel Edward should
have the satisfaction of being pursued by a
shameless hussy. I shall write to him this very
minute. I'll come to your room to inspect your
purchases immediately after I finish, shall I?" she
asked, bustling her still bemused sister out of the

room with her packages jammed helter-skelter in her arms.

At the door Elizabeth kissed her sister warmly. "I'll always be grateful to you for coercing my confidence today, Carina. If you had not, I might never have known that Edward loved me. I might eventually have married someone else just because it was expected and because I could not think of giving up the privilege of having children." She shuddered suddenly. "Oh, it does not bear thinking of. Thank you, Carina."

The door closed quietly on a radiant girl Carina hardly recognized as the cool, serene sister who had been her mentor for so long.

CHAPTER 11

It was nearly 10:00 P.M. as the two gentlemen attired in impeccable evening dress sauntered down Brook Street, bound for the imposing town residence of Mrs. Horatio Lethbridge. She was holding one of her popular musical evenings and Gavin, who was no mean performer on the pianoforte himself, was looking forward to an enjoyable time. He was not so sure about Ned though, giving the large, quiet man at his side a thoughtful glance. Ned was not himself tonight, preoccupied and jumpy as a cat on hot bricks. He wondered if anything was amiss on his estate.

"Did you find things in good trim at Shavelings?"

"Oh, yes; I stayed longer than I anticipated, though, between going over the accounts with my baliff and supervising some late planting. I have not spent much time at home the past couple of years and every now and again it is vital to move right in and reacquaint myself with the schedule. Jameson's a good man, though. I don't worry about the place while he's around. You don't spend much time even at your principal estate, do you?"

"Not too much, but the Cedars has the advantage of being just over an hour away. I can pop in for a morning every other week or so and be brought right up-to-date."

"Yes, that is an advantage. It takes me better than two and a half hours to reach Shavelings, so I generally stay overnight when I go down."

"How long were you there this time?"

"Four days. Got back scarcely an hour ago. Good thing you were late tonight. Just had time to grab something to eat and jump into these clothes before you arrived." And time to send around a note in answer to the extraordinary request for a meeting contained in a note from Elizabeth discovered amongst his post. He unconsciously patted the pocket over his heart where this missive now reposed. The news that Miss Raven was out for the evening was not unexpected, but as her note had been delivered the day after his withdrawal from town, he had not wished to let slip any remote chance of finding her immediately. For what reason could she possibly wish to see him? His brain had seethed with conjecture as he mechanically donned the apparel laid out by his valet and staved off starvation by masticating and swallowing heaven knew what. He would be spending the long evening in a fever of impatience, willing the time to pass quickly till the morning when he could reasonably hope to find her at home.

Gavin's voice broke into his abstraction and he smiled at his friend. "Er, what did you say? Afraid I was woolgathering."

Gavin's eyes were curious but he said mildly, "We are going to be late. By all means let us at-

tempt to slide in without attracting Mrs. Lethbridge's reproachful eyes."

"Lord, yes, she takes these musicales so seriously."

They had now entered the big oak door and
were divesting themselves of hat and gloves. Edward gave a regulatory tug to his hastily tied
cravat, Gavin waved away the porter, and they began to ascend the staircase, aware of the silence
of the house.

Suddenly a lovely soprano voice drifted down
to them. Gavin paused. "I was not aware Mrs.
Lethbridge meant to import some of the opera
company tonight. Thought she was featuring that
Viennese chap playing his own compositions on
the pianoforte."

"That is not a professional singer. Unless I'm
vastly mistaken, Carina is singing."

The instant illumination of Edward's habitually
quiet features by an expression beyond mere
pleasure was supremely irritating to Gavin and he
answered sharply:

"Nonsense! Did you see *Le Nozze di Figaro*
when it was presented at Haymarket a couple of
years ago?" At Edward's negative shake he continued with an upward gesture of his head: "That
aria is from the third act and is a very dramatic
and demanding proposition, way beyond a child
like Carina, no matter how good her voice." He
looked challengingly at Edward who said meekly,
but with a gleam of pure amusement lighting the
hazel eyes:

"You are probably correct, dear boy. Certainly
beyond a child. Shall we go up and see?"

Gavin shot him a suspicious look but did not reply. Unfortunately their entrance into the combined drawing rooms was not so unobtrusive as they could have wished. Granted the vast majority of the fifty or sixty guests was paying rapt attention to the performer, but their hostess spotted them immediately and detached herself from the small group she was sitting with at the back of the room. She glided softly over to welcome the latecomers with faintly excessive graciousness. Edward sent a humorous glance in Gavin's direction and good-naturedly allowed himself to be drawn apart by Mrs. Lethbridge who, as luck would have it, had not noticed her other guest's abstraction. For Gavin, unaware of Edward's good deed, unaware even of the presence of his hostess after his first cursory greeting, was standing as though hypnotized, his astounded gaze riveted to a space beside the beautiful japanned pianoforte where Carina shone in a blaze of light from an enormous silver candelabrum on the pianoforte and a crystal chandelier overhead. Her hair flashed fire to rival the candle flames and her pale yellow gown, embroidered all over with gold threads, exuded a radiance matched by her shimmering beauty as she stood with simple composure singing the countess's hauting lament "Dov'è sono i bei momenti." They had missed much of the initial regret in the aria, and now the mood of the music was changing, the lyrical voice soared in a beautiful expression of hope for a change in the unfaithful count. Powerful and true, her voice rose to the triumphant finale, successfully conveying to her listeners the courage and steadfast character of Countess Almaviva. As she finished there was a sound of a general release of breath from the enthralled audience before a really appreciative storm of applause broke out.

Gavin did not emerge like the rest from the spell of the emotions created by this tiny young girl with the exquisite voice and masterly dramatic technique. Hands at his sides he continued to stare at the now smiling and curtsying girl, knowing yet unwilling to accept the simple, overwhelming truth that his pleasant existence was now forever changed by the presence of this small, vital girl, young but *not* a child. Here was everything necessary to his future happiness, everything before tonight was the dead past, however much he might prefer it otherwise, and Carina was all of the future.

Carina was thanking her accompanist and had not yet noticed Gavin's presence, but Elizabeth, whose loving attention had been all on her sister during the performance, had turned to survey the audience immediately afterward for their response to her sister's singing. She spotted Gavin almost at once. Gavin had been made embarrassingly aware that Carina had witnessed his initial reaction to her sister's beauty, so perhaps it was all to the good that he was totally unaware in this moment of revelation that Miss Elizabeth Raven was watching him, wearing an expression that on anyone one degree less beautiful could only have been described as smug.

Both had schooled their features to pleasant social masks a moment later when Elizabeth joined Gavin in the rear of the room, giving up her place to the gentleman who had played Carina's accompaniment. Carina, who had not yet seen Gavin, was seated with him as they waited for the young pianist-composer from Vienna to settle himself at the pianoforte. Elizabeth smiled serenely at Gavin and murmured a conventional greeting, then seemed to give her entire attention to the front of the room.

"Are you not interested in my reaction to Carina's singing?" he said, quizzing her with wicked blue eyes.

"Yes, of course, but what can you say to her sister except that it was a magnificent performance?"

"It was a magnificent performance," he assured her with a smile, then continued seriously, "You must know her voice is exceedingly beautiful, but I confess I am amazed at her dramatic powers and sheer theatrical technique. Such accomplishment in one so young is extraordinary."

"She has never sung better," agreed Elizabeth.

"Who was the fellow who accompanied her?" he asked with elaborate casualness.

"Lord Marmaduke Pevency." Her tone matched his. "We met him last week at Lady Moreton's. Carina sang there too. He is a great admirer of her voice. I usually accompany her but he begged to be allowed the honor."

"He shows good taste," Gavin put in smoothly, inwardly cursing a fate that had kept him from being present upon any previous occasions when Carina had sung. He had not failed to note with extreme repugnance the cow-eyed glances being sent Carina's way by young Lord Marmaduke Pevency.

Because her sister had made such a sensation and she herself was not yet aware of Edward's presence, Elizabeth, who was nearly as accomplished on the pianoforte as Carina was vocally, settled back to unabridged enjoyment of the superlative performance of the young Viennese. Not so her companion, however. Between innate resentment at discovering the unpalatable truth of his feelings for Carina and unthinking jealousy of the worthy young man who was currently enjoying her friendly attentions, he was too full of conflict to be in a receptive frame of mind for music, however excellent. Nor, after the penitential performance, was he immediately rewarded for his patience by an interval of Carina's exclusive company. She was surrounded by persons eager to congratulate her or persuade her to grace their musical entertainments.

He escorted Elizabeth to the buffet and later, in obedience to his hostess's imperative summons, was presented to a group of visiting relatives from Yorkshire, a treat that, in his present state of unresolved tension, he had some difficulty in appreciating properly.

Elizabeth meanwhile was chattering with more than her customary animation to an extremely appreciative and admiring masculine audience when she felt a tingling along her spine and turned slowly to encounter Edward's grave look directed on her with nail-point precision. His eyes looked their question as the slow color warmed her cheeks and the harebell eyes softened. She excused herself from her conversation and slowly approached the tall man who came forward almost reluctantly and extended his hand, though his eyes never left her beautiful countenance.

"I regret I was away when your note arrived. I shall wait upon you tomorrow morning unless you care to tell me now what I may have the honor of doing for you?"

He had kept her hand in his throughout this formal speech. Elizabeth made no effort to remove hers from the warm grip but neither could she make an effort to speak for the moment. The question in his eyes deepened as she looked lingeringly, almost hungrily at the dear face.

"I . . . I'm not sure that I can now," she whispered.

He felt the trembling in her fingers and concern wiped out the question in the hazel eyes. "Perhaps if we were to go into the book room over there we might manage a few minutes of privacy."

He led her to the small, book-lined room and closed the door, leaning his broad shoulders against the panels as he regarded her in silence. Elizabeth knew what she wished to do and say but found her courage had oozed away during the agonizing three-day wait between the delivery of her letter and Edward's appearance. She looked at him helplessly, mutely begging his assistance.

He gave it in his kind fashion. "You know you may say anything to me, Elizabeth, and that I am yours to command."

She gripped her fingers tightly together in front of her and took a shallow breath. "Carina told me that you asked Papa's permission to address me two years ago. Edward, he never told me, I never knew." She watched the color slowly drain away from his face, leaving his eyes burning dark spots. "Do you still want me?" she finished in a whisper.

"Want you?" His voice was harsh with repression. "I could die from wanting you!" He had covered the distance between them in two strides and now swept her into his arms. She lifted her face for his kiss in the most natural way possible and then all thought vanished for an enchanted interval.

Their love had been ruthlessly cut down before flowering and been driven underground, but this had only served to strengthen the roots. Without any signs to sustain it, they had each recognized it and kept it alive, and now they were reaping a harvest of delight. Edward, that gentlest of men, was crushing her in an embrace that bade fair to crack her ribs, and Elizabeth, that model of propriety, was clinging to her lover with an unladylike abandon that would have called forth instant censure from her aunt. When at last Edward raised his head and loosened his hold, it was merely to the degree that would enable him to study the radiantly beautiful face gazing rapturously up at him.

"Beloved girl. I had stopped hoping, I think."

"So had I." She shuddered. "Oh, Edward, if it had not been for Carina I might never have known." She dropped her head on his shoulder and his lips moved over her forehead and the golden hair.

"Let us not dwell on that prospect, my love. Elizabeth . . ."

At the change in his voice she glanced up questioningly.

"Your father will not have changed his mind, you know."

She put her fingers firmly against his lips to prevent any chivalrous utterings. "We need not wait one day beyond my twenty-first birthday," she said with perfect steadiness. "Papa's reasons are all worldly ones; they need not concern us."

"I have no fortune to offer you, merely an independence. I am no better than Edgemere."

"Edward, I wished to marry you before I inherited Grandfather's fortune. Why should the money change that?" she asked with perfect feminine reasoning.

His smile was rueful but he cupped her chin in one large hand and said softly, "You do know that worldly considerations play no part in what I feel for you? You believe I love you?"

She nodded, coloring shyly under the passionate intensity of that regard, and he kissed her once more, very gently this time, before releasing her with a regretful sigh.

"Someone might enter at any time. We had best join the rest of the company. Do you think you might contrive to look like a girl who has *not* been kissed, my darling?" he teased.

She blushed again. "If you promise not to look at me like that. Oh, Edward, I do love you so."

"That is no way to stop me from looking 'like that,' sweetheart," he laughed. "Shall we find Carina and tell her?"

"She will not need telling," Elizabeth countered gaily as they returned to the supper room.

They did not find Carina immediately, however, but were approached by various enthusiasts either requesting the favor of Elizabeth's opinion on the composer or desirous of expressing their own.

At that moment a puzzled Carina was being conducted toward the book room by a somewhat nervous Sir Anthony Mercer. As he started to close the door she said casually, "Better not, Tony. We can be private and out of view here without chancing talk. That's better. No one can say the door is shut, but we won't be visible over here by the fireplace. Come, sit down."

She patted the brocaded sofa upon which she was perched, but for the moment he ignored the invitation and stood staring down into the fireplace. Carina waited patiently. It was a relief to escape for a moment from the press of people anxious to praise her performance, though she was tremendously excited and buoyed up by the spontaneous admiration her singing had evoked. Carina was too honest to deprecate her gift. She loved to sing and knew she could have made it her profession had she had not been born into a level of society where such a pursuit was impossible. After a thrilling experience like tonight's triumph, the firmly repressed hankerings in this direction reared their heads once more, so she welcomed this quiet interlude with congenial company. Tony did not look like being particularly congenial at the moment, however. He was obviously in the grip of some powerful but rather uncomfortable emotion judging by the way he tugged at his cravat and ran a smoothing hand over his well-behaved light brown hair that never needed smoothing.

"What's wrong, Tony?" she asked sympathetically. "Can I help?"

He looked up at that with a self-mocking little twist of his mouth. "You can, but will you?" he muttered, approaching her slowly. He held out his hands and mechanically she extended hers, allowring him to pull her upright. Once on her feet he retained her hands. After a tentative unsuccessful twist to release them, Carina remained quiescent, looking inquiringly up at her friend's eager face.

"I never meant to ask you yet, but you are so beautiful tonight, and you sang like an angel. Somehow I cannot remain silent any longer. Carina, Will you . . . do you think you could bring yourself to marry me?"

Carina was silent, but the absolute shock on her face goaded her companion to hurry into further speech. "You do not have to give me an answer now, but why should you look so surprised? We are the best of friends. You know I would do anything for you. You must have guessed that I . . . that I . . ." He broke off as she was slowly shaking her head.

"How could I have guessed that you might wish to marry me? We have been such good friends. You said you did not mean to ask me. Do you not see, everything is strange tonight—you have never heard me sing before—I seem different to you. But tomorrow everything will be as it was. I shall be just your friend Carina once more . . ."

"No, Carina, you may shut your eyes and pretend tonight never happened but you cannot change the fact that I love you. Let me finish please," he begged as her lips parted to utter an involuntary protest. "I have loved you from the beginning but you seemed so young, it would have been ridiculous to speak earlier. It's true you do seem different tonight. No doubt that is why I could no longer remain silent. I realize you have been in the habit of thinking of me as a friend only. But may I hope that in future you will try to consider me as a husband?"

Carina had never felt more miserable in her young life. She was very fond of Tony and she shrank from giving him pain. It was an effort to produce the words that had to be said.

"I am so sorry, Tony," she managed at last, "but I do not love you. I could not marry without love."

The very real regret in her face convinced him where words might not. "I won't press you. I think I knew really," he shrugged unhappily, "but I had to try. Please believe though that I shall be of the same mind if you should ever decide . . ."

"Oh, Tony," she whispered, "pray do not . . . but I shall always be your very good friend." Impulsively she placed her hands on his shoulders and, reaching up, pressed her lips to his in a brief salute.

Gavin Delawney, who had entered the room at that instant, witnessed only this fleeting contact and drew in his breath, almost wincing as if the anticipated blow would strike him instead of Sir Anthony. It did not come.

Sir Anthony walked quickly out of the room without acknowledging Gavin, if indeed he was aware of his presence. Gavin glanced from his retreating back to the averted face of the girl standing by the sofa gazing unseeingly into the fire.

"May I be of assistance?" he offered austerely.

"I . . . I beg your pardon?" Carina turned to face him fully, though her mind obviously still dwelt elsewhere.

"Has Mercer been annoying you? Do you wish me to speak to him?"

"Speak to him?" she echoed stupidly.

Gavin's mouth tightened unpleasantly but he

answered with heavy patience. "For daring to kiss you." He approached her silently and stood looking down at her expressionlessly.

"Good heavens, no. Besides he did not kiss me, I kissed him." Her thoughts were still lingering on the sad little interview just concluded and she answered more or less at random.

Random or not, these unfortunate words produced an immediate and unexpected reaction. Gavin's eyes glittered dangerously as he said with suave cruelty, "Well, since you are so free with your favors, why should I be left out?"

Before Carina knew what he was about, she found herself seized roughly. Her two hands were clipped neatly behind her back by one of his and the other held the back of her head in a viselike grip, forcing her face to tilt toward his. The ensuing contact was more of an assault than a kiss in the beginning. Punishment rather than love was the motivation and this Carina recognized dimly. She struggled instinctively with frantic impotence to break away from the suffocating hold. Curiously enough it never occurred to her to punch her aggressor, though he had certainly provided against that eventuality, nor did she kick out as she undoubtedly would have done to a stranger. Her reactions were composed of equal parts rage and chagrin and sheer disbelief, though she had no coherent thought except to free her mouth from that bruising contact. Gradually even this remnant of intelligent behavior disappeared as the nature of the kiss changed. The smoothness of her skin, the sheer heady feminine aura of the girl pressed close to him had its insidious effect on Gavin, and his mouth softened and began to move

over hers lingeringly, almost gently. The effect on
Carina was at first an instinctive cessation of her
struggles, followed by an alarming sense of
weakness in her lower limbs. Whether her depravity
eventually might even have countenanced
outright cooperation was to remain an unanswered
question, however, for at this stage some
instinct of awareness caused Gavin to turn his
head. Carina was incapable of movement, but her
dazed glance fell upon a familiar figure exiting
quickly from the room. For a second longer she
needed the support of Gavin's hands on her
arms, but his next words stiffened her spine most
effectively.

"We seem to have been observed," he drawled
hatefully. "Naturally you have my formal offer of
marriage, ma'am."

Carina gasped as though she had been slapped.

"Just like that! To make an honest woman of
me, I apprehend?"

"Something of the sort," he admitted with a
tiny laugh.

If Carina had not been seeing everything
through a haze of fury, she might have noted that
his voice was caressingly soft and there was a
gentle smile curving his lips, not to mention a
warm glow in the brilliant blue eyes. But she was
too intent upon achieving a cloak of coldness to
cover her trembling rage to study his expression.

"Now I suppose you are waiting for the words
that will make you the happiest of men?" she inquired
with acid sweetness.

He had the supreme audacity to laugh.

"Very well, here they are. Since the person who
witnessed that flagrant attack"—she positively rel-

ished the sight of those dark red brows drawing together—"was Sir Edward Lynton who would never dream of breathing a word of it to anyone, you will be greatly relieved to hear that I hereby decline your most obliging offer. Good night, sir." She swept him a deep curtsy but her subsequent intention of sweeping out of the room was thwarted by the simple expedient of a hand on her arm, a none too gentle hand that spun her around to face him.

"Don't be a little fool; Ned is only human. This regrettable incident cannot be hidden for long. You must marry me; you have no choice."

She gritted her teeth but said with the coolness she intuitively knew he resented, "Nonsense, Edward would never do anything to hurt me."

"Why?" he snapped. "Is he also the recipient of your favors."

If it gave him satisfaction to see her lose control, the next moment must have been supremely satisfying. Carina did not use her fist this time but she put all her strength into an open-handed blow across his face. The sickening sound of contact finally pierced the cloud of rage. Horror and regret for hurting Gavin mingled with fury at his behavior turned to numb misery, but she was still too angry to apologize. Wordlessly she backed away from him, trying not to see the livid patch on his cheek, then spun about and almost ran out of the room.

Gavin took one hasty step in pursuit, then glanced frowningly in the glass over the fireplace. The angry red mark left by her blow confirmed his suspicion that he would compromise her more surely by an appearance directly in her wake, looking as he now did, than by anything guessed at from her agitation, not to mention branding himself a cad. Besides, she might have entirely regained her composure by now. Certainly she had proved more than a match for his stampeding tactics until that final insult. What a cursed, stupid fool he had been to try to take advantage of the situation created by that impulsive kiss. As if he would wish her unwilling compliance. Fundamentally he had no doubts at all that Carina was destined to be his, that in time she would come to him willingly, joyfully. One hand ruefully explored his still-stinging cheek as he wondered how long he'd be trapped in this room before his appearance would pass scrutiny. She swung a potent arm for such a tiny creature. Well, none of the milk-and-water misses paraded for his approval in the last few years had pleased him. If he would covet a fiery little shrew, he must make up his mind to a less than peaceful existence.

Strangely enough the contemplation of a disturbed future scarcely seemed to have a sobering influence on him. The chattering trio who drifted into the book room shortly thereafter to discover its lone occupant perusing a large tome, wondered what could possibly be so entertaining about a volume of sermons to bring a look of pleased anticipation to the young man's face.

Meanwhile Carina, leaving the scene of two intensely wearing emotional interludes, almost literally ran into Sir Edward Lynton standing just outside the doorway. It was not until much later when she could reexamine the events of the evening in a level-headed manner that she realized Edward must actually have been standing sentry duty to prevent any inopportune discovery of Gavin and herself. At the time she only knew a fervent gratitude that it was Edward and not someone who would expect rational conversation from her who caught her gently by the arms, arresting her flight. His narrow-eyed scrutiny of her wan face brought forth a sudden rush of color as she recalled that Edward had witnessed that unspeakable embrace and, for all she knew to the contrary, might well have heard the bitter exchange that followed, though she trusted they had kept their voices low. She stared at him mutely but he merely said quietly,

"Ah, that's better. For a moment you looked alarmingly pale, my dear. Come, your sister has something to say to you."

Relief that he was apparently prepared to ignore the scene he had witnessed flooded through her, but it needed another moment before his words penetrated her self-absorption. She had mechanically allowed him to lead her away, but now she paused and an expression of real delight animated her features.

"Oh, Edward, Liza has spoken to you. Is everything settled?" She gurgled with laughter. "How idiotish of me, to be sure. Of course it is; one look at you would tell a blindman. I do hope I am the first to wish you happy."

"You are, my dear. Who else should we wish to share our happiness, if not you? We owe you a lot, Carina." He hesitated, giving her an intent look, "If I can be of service to you in any way, you have only to command me." For a second she was afraid he might say more, but evidently her suddenly evasive expression impressed him and he fell tactfully silent. Dear Edward, always so understanding.

Carina went right up to her sister who was talking to old Mrs. Mendlebury and her spinster daughter and gave her a look sparkling with mischief as she said innocently,

"Edward says you wish to tell me something, Liza. How do you do, Mrs. Mendlebury? How nice to see you. Good evening, Miss Mendlebury, it has been an age since we have met." She smilingly accepted their plaudits on her singing and agreed that the Viennese composer's works were quite delightful, and yes, he did have charming manners also, quite a personable young man indeed.

Mrs. Mendlebury's avid features sharpened and she interrupted her daughter's timid comments: "I fear we are preventing Miss Raven from speaking privately to her sister, my dear Lucy."

"Not at all, Mrs. Mendlebury. I merely intended to pass on a compliment on her performance to my sister." Elizabeth smiled her sweet, serene smile, and except for a quiet air of content that could have been due to her sister's success, there was nothing out of the ordinary about her appearance. Mrs. Mendlebury glanced swiftly at Sir Edward, who stood with an air of civil attention, and swallowed her disappointment while herding her cowed daughter off to say their farewells to their hostess.

Carina twinkled at her sister. "Have you nothing more interesting to say to me than a second-hand compliment then, Liza?"

"Nothing you do not already know, Dearest." And now if Mrs. Mendlebury's curious eyes had chanced to scrutinize her latest victim, they could not have failed to discern the quiet glow of happiness enriching her loveliness.

A different but equally shrewd observer was noticing her radiance at that moment, however. As Carina turned away with the intention of finding her aunt so they might prepare to depart, she came face to face with his lordship, the Earl of Edgemere. She could not quite account for the little *frisson* of fear that traveled down her spine at the discovery of his furious concentration on her sister and Edward who still stood together, but she had to acknowledge it. She and the earl bowed formally to each other and moved off in different directions. He had guessed, of course, but nothing he could do would alter the situation. She dismissed him from her thoughts with a mental shrug and resumed her search for her aunt.

It had been a surprising evening all told, she reflected soberly in the carriage a few moments later, not the least of which surprises was Miss Silverdown's reaction to her niece's news. For this lady, with a perspicacity born of intimate knowledge and lifelong love of Elizabeth, was not in the least astonished to hear she and Edward wished to marry.

"Did Papa tell you Edward offered for me?" demanded Elizabeth, somewhat hurt to think her aunt had kept this knowledge from her all this time.

"No, my dear. Matthew never condescended to tell me anything of importance, but I have eyes in my head and I cut my wisdoms many years ago. When a girl refuses as many eligible offers as you have, the reason can only be another man. Except for Lord Byron, who strikes me as sadly unsteady with nothing more than his handsome face to recommend him, Edward seemed to be the only man of our acquaintance who had not dangled after you. I could not judge you so sadly lacking in discernment as to prefer Lord Byron to our dear Edward. I did not know that Edward had approached your father, but after noticing the way he looked at you when he thought himself unobserved, I assumed there was some impediment that prevented him from following his inclinations."

"And you never said anything to Liza or Edward or anyone?" Carina was awestruck at this new picture of her garrulous, gossip-loving aunt refraining from discussing what must have been an intriguing situation.

"There are some circumstances in which well-meant interference can be fatal," said Miss Silverdown seriously, "and in this instance neither Elizabeth nor Edward gave any indication of willingness to encourage confidence, so I thought I had best remain blind and hope that something might occur that would bring matters to a head."

"Oh, Aunt," cried Elizabeth remorsefully, "dearest Aunt, I simply could not confide in anyone, do you not comprehend? I thought Edward was indifferent to me. That sort of unhappy situation can only be kept secret."

At this Miss Silverdown sought to reassure her distressed niece that she did indeed understand and commended the strength of character that preferred suffering alone to involving one's nearest and dearest with one's complaints.

Carina smiled wryly in the dimness of the carriage and wondered if she possessed the requisite strength of character to suffer tonight's disasters alone. Part of her was longing to pour out the entire story of the evening's indignities into Elizabeth's sympathetic ears, but for Tony's sake, and even more for Gavin's (not that the latter deserved the slightest consideration; indeed the reverse was true), she felt an equal reluctance to divulge the happenings in the book room. It was not a case of least said, soonest mended, because she knew intuitively that her former happy relationships with both young men were irretrievably altered as a result of the evening's scenes. She sighed deeply and resolved on silence as her best course, at least for the present. Thank heavens Liza's happiness was now assured. This would serve to give her chaotic thoughts a more pleasant direction.

CHAPTER 12

Gavin and Edward walked back toward Edward's lodgings together, but this time it was the younger man who seemed abstracted. Edward refrained from making conversation for the most part but eventually his soft, tuneless whistling reached his self-absorbed companion.

"You look like a man whose suit has prospered," he tossed carelessly, and promptly regretted the unfortunate remark that gave Ned the opportunity to retort:

"And you have the appearance of a man whose suit has not prospered."

In view of the fact that Ned had witnessed the embrace in the book room, this bald statement was loaded with portent, and for Carina's sake Gavin was forced to reply.

"No, she turned me down." His tone was most unencouraging but his friend ignored the warning.

"You did ask, then?"

Gavin turned on him with a snarl. "What do you think I am? If you imagined I'd play the cad with an innocent like Carina, then you want your cork drawn." He stopped abruptly under one of the new gas streetlights. The dangerous glitter in his eyes did not impress his companion, however.

"I did not think it," he said mildly, "but Carina did not act like a girl who had just received a flattering offer when she emerged from the book room; she was upset." Gavin began to walk on without replying to this invitation, so after a moment Ned went on: "What happened to the vaunted Delawney address?"

The younger man went a dull red at this taunt but refused to be baited. "You are mighty curious about something that is none of your affair."

"You are mistaken. Anything to do with Carina is my affair."

Gavin stopped again and wheeled to face his good friend with a bleak expression. "Are you trying to tell me that you and Carina—"

"Good lord, no, but she has always been just like my own sister." He hesitated, watching Gavin expel a drawn breath. "I don't mind telling you, but it is to go no further. My suit did prosper. Elizabeth has done me the honor of accepting my offer."

"Elizabeth!" Gavin was thunderstruck. "You never gave each other a glance. I thought you had a *tendre* for Carina." He coughed loudly, wishing he could call back the hasty words, but Edward merely laughed, albeit a trifle grimly.

"Her father refused me two years ago and will no doubt refuse me again. We shall have to wait till Elizabeth comes of age, so there will be no announcement yet. And I do have a deep affection for Carina. Anyone who hurts her will answer to me."

Gavin's hand rubbed his cheek absently. "That young lady can take care of herself, never fear."

Edward's quick intelligence had appreciated the gesture, but with real nobility he subdued the laughter bubbling up. His nobility of character did not prevent a mild jibe at his slightly disconsolate friend, however.

"I wondered when you would make the startling discovery that Carina is not a child."

"No, she's not," Gavin agreed shortly, recalling, not for the first time in the last hour, that all-too-brief magical moment after Carina had stopped struggling in his arms, when he would have taken his oath that she had melted closer into his embrace and the soft lips were beginning to respond to his. Better not to dwell on that for the present. He gave Edward a glance of acute distaste.

"You chose the worst possible moment for your appearance."

"I know, old chap, beastly clumsy of me. Accept my most humble apologies."

"I'm damned if I will," declared Gavin, pardonably incensed by the undercurrent of laughter in his friends's voice. "I'm not so sure I want you for a brother-in-law after all. By the way I believe I neglected to offer my congratulations." He thrust out his hand. "You know I wish you happy, Ned. She's a lovely girl."

"Thank you. Do I gather from your previous remark that you still have the intention of becoming my brother-in-law? You do not regard the lady's decision as irrevocable then?"

"What's irrevocable is the fact that Carina is mine and I intend to make her admit it," his friend stated flatly with what must have seemed like an excess of confidence surely in the circumstances. Edward however evidently found nothing pot-valiant about it.

"I'm in your corner, dear boy, but if I know Carina, she will lead you a merry dance."

Gavin waved that gloomy prognostication aside. "What do you know of Lord Marmaduke Pevency? She's attached him of late."

"Nothing but the most complimentary. Young, but definitely up to snuff. Good seat, good hands, shows to advantage in the ring, took honors at Cambridge, doesn't want for sense and seems to be popular with the female sex." As Gavin ground his teeth audibly he added with intent to comfort, "It's my guess that one of your rivals got his *congé* tonight, though. I'd wager my last monkey Mercer popped the question and was refused. Saw him coming out of the book room looking blue as megrim. That's why I came in so inopportunely. Had a hunch I'd find Carina there. Didn't realize she had 'em queuing up, of course," he added apologetically, slanting a glance at his friend who had an arrested look in his eyes as the light from torches outside Edward's lodgings washed over his lean, muscular form.

Gavin made no reply and bid the tall man a rather absent good night after refusing an invitation to sample his brandy. He walked rather slowly toward Cavendish Square, turning this latest information over in his mind. If what Ned suggested had actually happened, it might account for Carina's abstracted air of *tristesse*. Certainly her manner had been far from flirtacious despite admitting that she had done the kissing in that wretched tableau he had witnessed, and heaven knew he himself had been utterly unsuccessful in engaging her in the mildest of flirtations. What had he thought, then, when he had entered the book room in time to see that fleeting kiss? He was compelled to the tardy though inexorable conclusion that his own actions had been in no way motivated by any rational thought process. There had always been the nagging little idea that Carina might care more for Mercer than she acknowledged, and the sight of the two of them together coming so soon upon his own realization of what she meant to him had triggered a moment of blind jealousy coupled with a desire to punish the one who unwittingly caused this uncomfortable feeling.

And what had that reckless act availed him? Carina was furious with him, and even if her present well-justified anger should quickly burn off, there would be a residue of embarrassment when next they met. He had proposed in the most insulting way possible, though he had not meant to insult her, and she had refused him in no uncertain terms. His arrival at his own home coincided with the realization that he faced an unpromising reception at Green Street when next he called. Yet as he entered his bedchamber shortly afterward, he could not quite regret that ungentlemanly embrace. She *had* responded; the knowledge was deep in his singing blood. Granted time and opportunity he could make her respond again.

Over the next few days, however, it became apparent that opportunity was just what he was not to be given. He called at Green Street daily to be told by the impassive Coleman that Miss Carina was out or the ladies were not receiving. He spent an interminable evening at Almack's vainly trying to achieve a moment of comparative privacy with Carina, but she excused herself from dancing with him and remained surrounded by eager swains for all the time that she did not actually spend on the dance floor.

He had been chilled to the marrow by her expressionless formality in refusing his invitation. Illogically, although he had been concerned about embarrassment attending their first meeting, he now resented the apparent absence of any such feeling on her part. Thanks to his pride and aided by a look of malicous enjoyment on the face of Lady Jersey who happened to be standing nearby at the time, he managed to conceal his own chagrin, though his set countenance as he turned away did not escape the watchful eye of Miss Elizabeth Raven. A wave of sympathy rose in her kind heart but she hesitated to approach him. Apart from a terse statement to the effect that she and Gavin had quarreled, Carina had offered no explanation of her recent determined avoidance of her good friend. Not knowing the reason for or substance of this quarrel, Elizabeth was fearful of showing disloyalty to her sister by acting on her sympathetic impluse to offer comfort to Gavin.

While she stood undecided the matter was taken out of her hands by the young man himself. Meeting her compassionate glance as he retreated, he immediately seized the opportunity to request a dance, then suggested they retire to an alcove to talk instead.

It soon developed that Gavin did not share Carina's reticence in divulging the nature of the quarrel. Willy-nilly Elizabeth was regaled with the entire tale and her support solicited in arranging a meeting with her recalcitrant sister.

Torn between amusement and sympathy she contrived to keep her countenance, realizing that neither reaction would endear her to the somewhat grim-faced young man facing her on the settee. It would be difficult to imagine anyone less loverlike, she mused thoughtfully. Though she had never doubted his sincere attachment to her sister, indeed she had clearly anticipated the way events were shaping long before either participant in this irregular love affair, at this moment it must be admitted that he seemed primed for a battle of wills and more determined to subdue than win Carina.

She frowned in concentration while Gavin waited with what patience his naturally impatient nature could command. When she spoke at last, her words were frank but bitterly disappointing to the action-minded Gavin.

"Please do not think I do not enter completely into your sentiments on this matter, but I would advise you not to build too much on what you imagine was Carina's reaction to your embrace." She calmly ignored the set jaw and slight scowl marring the usually genial features of this handsome young man. "Carina is very young and, unlike most girls, has given no thought at all to marriage, partially because she has long since been aware that her marriage portion is very small."

"I don't care if she hasn't a bean," he declared with some impatience.

"I believe you, but do you not see how this situation has colored her thinking on the matter of marriage? She came to town prepared to enjoy her season but in full expectation of returning permanently to Ravenshill. It will take time for her to accept that your suit is serious, especially after the way in which you say your offer was made." She paused delicately and Gavin reddened and shifted position uncomfortably.

"I know I was a brute, but I was so incensed to see her kissing that fellow that I lost my head. If Ned had not come in at that precise moment, I could have talked her around."

"Are you sure?" she inserted gently.

His jaw set even more stubbornly. "Yes. Oh, I know I sound like a coxcomb, but pray believe it isn't vanity. I just *know* that Carina is mine. If she doesn't know it yet I must convince her. Can you not persuade her to see me?"

In deference to his real unhappiness Elizabeth kindly refrained from pointing out that this knowledge was apparently of very recent date.

"Well, we are making up a party to go to Vauxhall on Friday. Edward did suggest that you be included but Carina would not agree. Lord Pevency is coming instead. However, Vauxhall is a big place. There might be some opportunity for a meeting." She said no more but he agreed somewhat grimly:

"I'll be there."

Neither was aware of the identity of the man a few feet away, standing with his back to them seemingly intent on opening his snuffbox. The Earl of Edgemere had paused there in time to overhear the last few remarks and now he strolled slowly away, his forehead creased in a thoughtful frown.

Gavin did notice the earl at Figg's Amphithe-atre the following night, however. Not that it was at all unusual to see a gentleman there witnessing a contest of strength and skill. A good number of the ton patronized Figg's to watch the latest chal-lengers' attempts to defeat the champions. Gavin's attention was drawn to the earl precisely because the latter's attention was so little focused on the match. He appeared to be absorbed in conversa-tion with an individual who bore none of the hall-marks of a gentleman, and at one point money changed hands. Of course the earl may have lost a wager to his unidentified companion, but some-thing about the stranger's general appearance teased at Gavin's memory. He was not quite un-known surely? Maneuvering for a clearer look, he approached the earl and greeted him politely. The earl returned the greeting coldly, but it was his companion's reaction that interested Gavin. He wondered if he detected a flicker of recognition in his eyes before he looked quickly away. The earl obviously had no intention of making the two men known to each other, and on closer inspection Gavin failed to recognize the man's features. His face was nondescript, nothing about it would stick in one's memory except that he had a faint but rather long scar that ran from his nose past the left side of his mouth. Gavin nodded a casual good night and turned away, mostly satisfied that the man was indeed a stranger although the scar tugged at his memory. It was too elusive to pin down, however, and he shrugged away the earl's taste for low company.

There was a sharp silence after Gavin left the

pair. The earl chewed his lip irritably, then said coldly to the other:

"That was unfortunate. His name is Delawney and he'll be somewhere about on Friday. See that you keep out of his way. I don't want anyone to be able to connect you with me. What's the matter?" His voice sharpened. "You look queer."

The other man was wiping his damp face with a none-too-clean handkerchief. "It's hot in here, that's all," he muttered. "I know what I'm to do. Just you be sure the rest of that money is waiting for me."

"Remember, I do not wish the girl to be hurt but they are nearly inseparable and I must have her removed from the scene for an hour or two. I'll point her out to you as early in the evening as possible."

CHAPTER 13

Carina was enchanted with Vauxhall. She had long anticipated her first visit to the delightful pleasure gardens and had been thrilled when Edward good-naturedly acceded to her wish to arrive by the water entrance. She would not have dared to give expression to this desire had their aunt been one of the party, for that lady was fearful of small boats, but Miss Silverdown had been laid up for several days with a feverish cold. She had now left her bedchamber and declined the tender ministrations of her nieces and Abby, but wisely refused to expose herself to the rigors of the night air so early in June. Consequently Sir Edward invited a middle-aged couple of his acquaintance to make up an unexceptional party of six. Fortunately Major and Mrs. Grierley put forward no objections to the proposed mode of travel so Carina was allowed her wish.

The busy Thames was lent mystery and beauty by a waning half-moon. The air was caressingly soft, and when they reached their destination, perfumed by flowers. There was little time to enjoy a stroll before the concert began, but Edward promised they might wander along the numerous walks following the supper he had ordered to be served in one of the booths.

The concert was well worth the appreciative attention Carina and the Grierleys were paying, but Elizabeth noted that as usual Lord Pevency's blue eyes kept straying to her sister, young and radiant in a sapphire blue gown of tucked French muslin with little puffed sleeves above which her shoulders gleamed whitely. He was certainly deeply smitten by Carina's charms and her sister generally appeared to enjoy his attentions unreservedly, though at this moment her interest was entirely upon the music.

Elizabeth turned to meet Edward's deep gaze and was conscious of a contentment beyond description. Though she attempted to focus her interest on the excellent selection of music offered during the next hour, neither her own newfound happiness nor her mild but bothersome concern for her sister's estrangement from Gavin was conducive to intelligent listening. While the string section rhapsodized over a choice section of Mozart, her mind strayed back to the scene with Carina before they had left home this evening. Knowing Carina could not have failed to notice her own tête-à-tête with Gavin at Almack's the other night, Elizabeth had confidently expected her sister to inquire about their conversation if only to ascertain what Gavin might have revealed concerning the events in the Lethbridge book room. To her consternation Carina completely ignored the incident in her spate of gay chatter following the assembly, nor did she refer to it or Gavin in the next couple of days, although Elizabeth gave her every opportunity to do so. Having tacitly promised Gavin to prepare Carina for a possible meeting with her impetuous but ungallant suitor, she realized with regret that it would be her unpleasant task to broach the subject to her strangely reticent sister before Friday evening. Though blessed with a natural tact, in the face of such secrecy on the part of her hitherto confiding sister, she felt her customary flair deserting her. When the deliberate mention of Gavin's name produced only stony-faced calm instead of the opening she sought, she finally threw diplomacy to the winds and admitted that Gavin had told her the whole story of their quarrel. Beyond stating dryly that she had refrained from mentioning the incident due to an apparently misplaced concern for Gavin's feelings, Carina exhibited a reluctance to discuss the situation which ordinarily Elizabeth's sense of delicacy would have respected. This very night, however, the spurned lover planned to present himself before his haughty beloved, and somehow (but never again!) she had allowed herself to be maneuvered into the uncomfortable position of devil's advocate. Sighing, she had plunged in reluctantly:

"Why will you not see him, Dearest, and allow him to make his apologies? It is not like you to be so unforgiving."

"I have no wish to see him again, ever."

"But, Carina, you two have been so very companionable during our entire stay in London. How can you permit a silly misunderstanding to ruin your friendship?"

Carina had gazed at her sister in patent disbelief.

"How can you call what happened a silly

misunderstanding? It was a violent quarrel. And Gavin is the one who spoiled our friendship, not I. He practically accused me of being *fast*. How can we ever be friends again after this?"

Knowing that Gavin's feeling for her sister was a world removed from friendship, Elizabeth had been quite at a loss for an answer to this question and had murmured evasively that it was only fair to see him and permit him to apologize.

"He may write me a letter of apology if his conscience troubles him," Carina had replied coldly, and Elizabeth had abandoned all further attempts at persuasion. Now, going over that uncomfortable conversation again to the sound of a Mozart sonata, she was struck by the omission on both sides of any mention whatever of Gavin's offer. Her eyes strayed thoughtfully to her sister still absorbed with the music. She was convinced Carina had had no inkling of Gavin's changing feeling toward her before that unfortunate proposal. Would any girl, least of all Carina with her complete lack of all personal vanity, believe in the sincerity of an offer made in such circumstances? The only possible answer was a clear negative. And did her sister wish that Gavin's proposal had been motivated by a real attachment to her? Studying Carina's rapt profile in search of evidence to support this theory proved fruitless. The only emotion Carina had displayed throughout was a cold anger that Gavin had misjudged her and spoiled their easy friendship. Elizabeth sighed soundlessly and covertly swept the assembled audience for a glimpse of Gavin, but could spot no dark red head. Just as well perhaps if he elected not to present himself tonight. Carina's present mood could only be described as unpropitious in the extreme.

During the excellent supper served to the party in the booth Edward had hired for the evening, Elizabeth was engulfed in the gaiety of the moment and soon abandoned her profitless speculation concerning her sister's affairs in favor of enjoying herself immensely. She watched the men devour prodigious amounts of the delectable pink ham that was a specialty at Vauxhall, convinced that after such a gargantuan repast none of their escorts would have the energy to wander round the numerous walks and alleys lit by a multitude of colored lights. In this prediction she was quite out however, for presently the men rose with every evidence of willingness to escort the ladies throughout the gardens. There was a fireworks display scheduled for midnight, but only Carina admitted to an interest in witnessing this spectacle. Naturally Lord Pevency was more than willing to accommodate her, and these two broke away from the others after a time, not wishing to wander too far afield so as to miss the beginning of the fireworks. In one of the small alleys they came upon a deserted bench and sat down to rest for a moment before making their way back to the site of the display. The conversation was desultory, for Lord Pevency was never loquacious and Carina was dreamily enjoying the fairy-tale atmosphere induced by the myriad colored lights. After a moment of silence on their part, a bird hopped cautiously out from under a rhododendron bush and came a bit closer. Carina held her breath and put an admonitory hand on her companion's arm, compelling his continued silence as she eagerly watched the approach of the tiny, curious bird. So engrossed was she in the beautiful little creature that she heard nothing save a strangled moan as she suddenly felt Lord Pevency's arm slip away from her hand. Turning in inquiry, her astonished eyes encountered her escort's form sliding silently from the bench.

"Duke!"

Automatically her hands went out to stop his fall but a movement in the shadows behind them caused her head to spin around, her eyes widening in alarm at the sight that met her. The man looming over the bench bit off a curse and applied himself to covering her mouth with a brutal hand before she could let out a sound. On the instant he was around the side of the bench, jerking her small form back against his chest. Carina clawed ineffectually at the fingers clamped tightly over her mouth and kicked out backward. Her satisfaction at making contact was all too brief, as with a startled grunt her assailant swept her off her feet and, carrying her under one arm as though she were a loaf of bread, proceeded farther down the alley which proved to lead to one of the small summerhouses dotted about the grounds. Carina, desperate to attract someone's attention, could hear faint laughter and voices but no one ventured near the small building. She was pummeling her captor wildly with both fists, but though he swore softly and continuously under his breath, he never broke his stride until he reached the summerhouse. He entered and dropped his breathless, squirming victim with dispatch onto a bench against a wall. Whipping out a scarf from his pocket, he swiftly tied it around her mouth to keep her quiet, then slumped back against the wall to catch his breath before attempting to tie up as nasty a little wildcat as it had ever been his misfortune to tangle with. He never took his eyes off the huddled form as he dashed the sweat from his forehead with the back of his sleeve, but it was a few seconds before he realized his task would no longer be such an effort. For the girl was utterly motionless now and for an instant his blood froze, then reaching reluctantly down to turn her, he felt her breath upon his hand. Relieved that she had merely swooned or maybe knocked herself out against the wall, he quickly proceeded to tie her ankles together and her hands behind her back. Then pausing only to check the tightness of the gag over her mouth, he quietly left the summerhouse and melted into the shadows.

Elizabeth strolled slowly on with Major and Mrs. Grierley, idly wondering who might have sent the message by a waiter that had caused Edward to excuse himself and head back toward the boxes a moment ago. Mrs. Grierley called her attention to a particularly beautiful tree, and after according it the homage of appreciative silence for a time, they meandered down yet another path.

"The gardens are not overcrowded tonight," commented Mrs. Grierley in some surprise after nodding to an acquaintance. "Generally one may meet half one's acquaintance here, but I vow Mrs. Elsworth is the first person I have recognized.

"That shower late this afternoon no doubt persuaded many people that the paths would be too wet for comfortable strolling," replied her husband, "but it seems to have dried up admirably."

"And," added Elizabeth smilingly, "unless my eyes deceive me two more of your friends are now approaching, the Misses Adderly."

Mrs. Grierley, who was a bit shortsighted, peered ahead of her. "Oh, yes, and I do believe Lady Moreton and her daughter are directly behind them."

The parties came together and exchanged friendly greetings and views on the concert. After a moment or two Major and Mrs. Grierley went on ahead slowly with the Adderlys, leaving Elizabeth to take a somewhat lingering farewell of Lady Moreton and the talkative Arabella. Her companions were just entering another path to the right and Elizabeth had increased her pace to catch them up when a voice behind her brought her up short.

"A moment, Miss Raven, if you please."

She turned somewhat reluctantly to face the Earl of Edgemere. "Good evening, my lord. I fear I shall have to hurry or I shall lose my friends."

His face was unusually serious. "Lynton sent me to find you." He hesitated and a trace of anxiety crept into her inquiring eyes. "It seems your sister has been taken ill suddenly and Lynton thought it best to escort her home immediately. Since I have my carriage here he has delegated me to act as your escort, knowing that you would wish to join Miss Carina at the earliest possible moment." As he spoke he had taken her elbow in a gentle hand and was leading her back along the path he had followed.

Elizabeth found her voice. "Carina ill! But it cannot be twenty minutes since she was last with me. Where is Lord Pevency?"

"He has gone with Lynton and your sister."

"What happened?"

"I fear I cannot tell you that. Lord Pevency was engaging a carriage and Lynton was supporting your sister. There was time for no more than a few words to request my assistance which, of course, I am only too pleased to render. Down this way," he added, guiding her to the carriage entrance where his beautifully built chaise awaited them, the steps already down. Quickly Elizabeth was assisted into it and the earl climbed in after her, closing the door firmly. The coachman had already cracked his whip over the team when Elizabeth said urgently:

"Stop! We cannot leave just yet. I have forgotten the Grierleys."

"They have already been notified," the earl said soothingly. "They may make their way back whenever they choose."

Elizabeth relaxed against the velvet squabs and released a long, quivering breath. She managed a wavering smile at the calm man sitting opposite her. The small lamp attached to the side of the carriage threw flickering shadows over his face.

"You have been most efficient, my lord. I am indeed grateful. You said Carina was being supported by Edward. Did you mean carried? Was she unconscious?"

There was the briefest pause. "No, she was able to walk with assistance though she looked quite pale."

"I cannot imagine what could have overtaken her. Except for the influenza last year, Carina has never been ill in her life."

"Might she have eaten something here that affected her?" he suggested easily.

Elizabeth's lovely forehead puckered slightly. "Nothing that the rest of the party did not also partake of. Besides, I believe Carina could digest rusty nails."

"Well, you shall be with her soon," the earl promised.

Conversation lapsed after this. Elizabeth was busy with her own thoughts and grateful for the earl's understanding silence. She had rather dreaded the thought of their first meeting since his importunate proposal, but he was being the soul of consideration and she felt more kindly disposed toward him than at any time in their acquaintance. Stealing a glance from under her gold-tipped lashes, she saw that her escort was wearing a preoccupied expression, his eyes fixed unseeingly on the corner of the carriage. Obviously she was not the only one with disturbing thoughts for company on this short drive. She noted idly that the velvet curtains had been drawn across the windows and she twitched the right-hand one back to peer out. Although beautifully sprung, it was evident by the slight sway of the chaise that they were traveling at a fast clip and should be quite near Green Street by now. It took a moment for her eyes to become adjusted to the silvered aspect of the greenery rushing past. Greenery! Not dwellings and city streets! The significance of a team of horses rather than a pair, dimly noted at the start of this trip, suddenly hit like a *coup de foudre.* For an instant panic rose in a flood tide, rendering her physically weak and trembling. She leaned her forehead against the glass, deriving some small comfort from its coolness while she fought down a nearly over-whelming impulse to give way to hysteria. Her teeth were tightly clamped together to prevent any betraying sound from escaping. She had been right to fear this man's determination to achieve his end, but she'd go willingly to the gallows be-fore allowing him the satisfaction of seeing her dread of him. She was aware that he was await-ing her reaction, and she knew her weakness, anyone's weakness, would delight him; he was that kind of man. This thought helped strengthen her voice as she asked with a desperate calm:

"Where are you taking me?"

Turning slowly she steeled herself to look at him without betraying herself and must have succeeded fairly well, for the malicious triumph she had expected to encounter in those light eyes was quickly replaced by a grudging admiration.

"My compliments, Elizabeth," he drawled, making her an ironic bow. "Not a scream, not a tear and no vapors, though I was prepared to en-counter any or all reactions. We shall deal very well together indeed."

"I do not recall making you free with my name, sir," she replied calmly, "and I am afraid we shall not deal together at all."

"Since we are going to become man and wife very shortly, I think you'll grant me the right to use your given name."

"You are mistaken, sir. We shall never be man and wife. I am betrothed to another."

"Lynton? Fortunately there has been no announcement. I wish to spare you any scandal I may, my dear, but when it is learned you have spent a night or better in my company, you will have no other course open to you."

Elizabeth's nails were driving into her palms with painful intensity but her face revealed none of her inner torment. She raised her beautiful eyes to his handsome, loathsome face.

"You cannot compel me to marry you."

"It distresses me to contradict a lady, my dear Elizabeth, but now it is you who are mistaken. An elopment that did not end in marriage would ruin you completely. You would no longer be received anywhere and twice your fortune would not serve to reestablish you."

"Oh, I am not doubting that you have it in your power to cause my social ruin by this *abduction*, but you will still not compel me to marry you." The quiet, almost expressionless tones and the serenity of her countenance seemed to provoke him in the extreme. The amber eyes narrowed and his lips thinned to a straight line.

"Do you think your beauty is so great that Lynton or any other man would marry you after this?" he sneered.

Elizabeth's steady blue gaze met and compelled his angry eyes as she answered with devastating conviction:

"I know nothing about beauty or other men, but even if you were to rape me, Edward would still marry me."

He lowered his eyelids to conceal the shock this

frank statement had produced but the sneer
remained in his voice.

"You are very sure of yourself, are you not?"

"I am very sure of Edward's love," she answered quietly. She could see that despite himself
he had been influenced by her absolute conviction. For the first time a shade of unease crossed
his face and she pressed her advantage.

"There is no point in going on with this, my
lord. I beg of you to return me to Green Street
and we will forget this ever happened." She held
her breath in the taut silence that followed, pray-
ing that she had convinced him of the folly of this
adventure. The sardonic mask was back, however,
and her heart dropped. Even before he spoke she
saw that she had failed.

"It was a good try, my dear, but I fear my
needs are so pressing that I am forced to call your
bluff, though you have my sincere admiration for
your gallant attempt to preserve your virtue for
Lynton. Once you have overcome your natural
disappointment in this turn of affairs, I feel sure
we shall suit admirably. In fact you quite intrigue
me. I never suspected that beneath that demure
facade dwelt a passionate nature. I shall quite enjoy teaching you to forget that cold fish, Lynton."

Elizabeth remained silent in the face of his
taunting, her head averted so that he should not
guess how perilously close she was to tears of
weakness. For a brief interval her hopes had risen
that she might convince him to abandon his desperate plan to coerce her acceptance of his offer.
Now her disappointment increased tenfold, and
she knew in silence lay her only hope of maintaining some composure during the ensuing ordeal.

The carriage, pulled by four strong thorough-breds, proceeded on its way, maintaining a good pace with the aid of the waning but clear moon. And now total silence engulfed the occupants.

CHAPTER 14

The fireworks display was reaching its colorful, noisy climax when Sir Edward Lynton at last came up to Mr. Gavin Delawney and said in some exasperation:

"I received your message. Why did you not wait at the booth for me to come? I was held up for a time by some friends, then I waited another ten minutes or so at the booth, hoping you would return instead of haring off to find me."

Gavin eyed his friend in some surprise. "I freely admit to being on the watch for you but I sent no message. Where is the rest of your party?"

"I left Elizabeth and the Grierleys walking along the paths. Carina and Pevency had wandered off to stay within range of the fireworks."

A particularly brilliant shower of orange and green lights lit up the sky momentarily then slowly faded to the accompaniment of a rapid volley of a sounds like gunfire, but the two men were alike impervious to its color and noise as they stared at each other. Edward was the first to break the short silence that had fallen between them.

"Did you happen to notice Carina and Pevency at the staging area?"

"No. The crowd was not overlarge tonight. I do not believe I could have missed them. Truth to tell I confidently thought to find Carina in the midst of the display."

"So she expected to be," Edward answered thoughtfully. "Perhaps Pevency persuaded her to linger in some quiet alley with him instead." His voice lacked conviction, however, and his friend said curtly:

"Carina is not the most persuadable girl I know. May I see that message?"

Edward handed it over and Gavin scanned the unrevealing note silently before returning it. "No attempt to emulate my hand, I see. Brought by a waiter, was it?"

"Yes. Shall we separate and comb the grounds for either or both parties? Like as not we shall meet them heading back this way before we have gone fifty yards."

Gavin nodded and the two men separated for a time. They met again in ten minutes at the intersection of two of the main walks. Gavin was alone but Edward was now accompanied by Major and Mrs. Grierley. Noticing the slight agitation of the latter, Gavin increased his pace and shot an interrogative look at Edward after a brief greeting to the older couple.

"They haven't seen Carina and Pevency since they left us shortly after supper. Elizabeth was with them until about fifteen minutes ago. She stopped to talk to Lady Moreton and Miss Moreton but was right behind them as they turned off that path over there into one of the alleys. When she did not catch them up in a minute or two, they retraced their steps, but she had vanished. They have been looking for her ever since."

Mrs. Grierley was wringing her hands. "I know she had the intention of following us directly because I looked back as we entered the alley and caught her eye. She nodded to me."

Gavin broke in to suggest the two parties separate again. This time he and Edward concentrated on the smaller alleys. On one leading from one of the summerhouses Edward stopped short, then hurried forward, and bending over, pulled at something lying under a rhododendron bush. A light blue gauze shawl shot with silver threads caught momentarily on a branch, then was retrieved by the grim-faced man.

"Carina was wearing this," he said briefly and made no demur when Gavin, his face pale in the tinted lights, took it from him and folded it carefully before putting it in his pocket.

Without a word they increased their pace, animated by a growing sense of urgency. Scarcely thirty feet ahead, the sight of a crumpled figure on the path in front of a bench caused them to break into a run. It was a man, and even as they reached him he was struggling to drag his body into a sitting position with the aid of one braced hand. The other was clamped shakily to the back of his head. His eyes which had been closed, flew open in alarm as he became aware of the two figures closing in on him from both sides.

"Pevency!" ejaculated Edward, seizing the arm on the ground and aiding him to his feet. "What happened? Where is Carina?"

Lord Pevency looked dazedly at the speaker.

Seeing he was quite unsteady Gavin aided Edward in seating him on the bench.

"I don't know what happened. Carina is not here?" Lord Pevency questioned, startled. "We were sitting on this bench, at least I suppose it was this bench, when I suddenly felt the most excruciating pain in my head. I . . . I must have lost consciousness. But Carina . . .?"

"Perhaps she went for help," Edward suggested.

"After first tossing her scarf under a bush?" snapped Gavin, and was gone on the words, running back the way they had come. Edward took one step after him then decided he had best remain with the still dazed young man for a while.

Gavin had remembered the little summerhouse. During his first cursory search of the gardens, he had not entered any of these structures, but something stronger than instinct was driving him toward this one. As he approached it, senses alert, he was convinced there was a rhythmic banging noise coming intermittently from inside, not loud, but insistent. Bursting in, he paused for the slightest second as his eyes adjusted to the gloom. A small figure, sprawled inelegantly on the bench against the far wall, turned large, apprehensive eyes in a white face toward the door, then closed those eyes as he quickly covered the few feet between them.

"Carina, are you hurt, my darling?" He was on his knees, working the handkerchief away from her mouth as he spoke, anxiety apparent in his tautly controlled features.

"No," said the victim with remarkable coolness, "and I am not your darling."

"No?" he said very softly with more than a hint of menace. He allowed himself one intent, exasperated stare before turning her gently over onto her side while he attempted to loosen the cords which bound her wrists together behind her back. He laughed without mirth.

"At least you have answered my question satisfactorily. You cannot be much damaged if you are ready to resume our quarrel."

"I am not hurt at all except that my head aches. I banged it when he threw me down on this bench." She added with a slightly incongruous attempt at dignity, "And I have no slightest intention of quarreling with you. How did you find me anyway?"

He was concentrating on the knots at her ankles now and did not answer immediately. The slight noise he had heard had been caused by Carina's feet striking the bench rhythmically, and the movements had served to tighten the knots.

"We found your scarf and Pevency. I had a hunch about this place. From my experience of you it is precisely the sort of place I would expect to find you tied up in." His voice was curt.

"Well!" she began indignantly, only to recall herself with a start, "Oh, good heavens! I had quite forgotten Duke for the moment. He was hurt. Is he all right? Has Elizabeth been worried about me?"

This time the silence lasted even longer. He succeeded in untying the cords and helped her gently to her feet. Seeing that her cramped position and tight bonds had left her somewhat shaky, he brushed aside her protests and, sweeping her up into his arms, proceeded to carry her back down the path up which he had dashed less than ten minutes before.

"Is Duke all right now? Has everyone been alarmed about me being missing?"

At this repetition of her previous question, Gavin's hands seemed to tighten about her. Keeping his gaze straight ahead he answered shortly:

"Pevency is conscious. I do not think he is badly hurt. You'll see him in a minute."

"Poor Elizabeth must be frantic."

He did not answer, and Carina's heartbeat, which had showed an alarming tendency to increase its rate since being gathered into his arms, speeded up still more.

"Gavin," she began uncertainly, but he looked down at her unsmilingly and said, "Hush, my darling, we are almost there. We'll talk then."

His unusual gentleness only served to escalate the rising sense of alarm tingling in her veins. As they came within sight of the deserted bench upon which she and Lord Pevency had so carelessly sat not so very many minutes ago, there seemed to Carina's bemused eyes to have gathered there a host of people who turned to stare as Gavin approached with his burden. The host resolved itself into four figures only, one of whom detached himself and strode to intercept the newcomers.

"Is she hurt?" Edward asked anxiously of Gavin, but it was Carina who answered somewhat impatiently:

"I am fine. Gavin insisted on carrying me because my legs were weak for a moment. Edward, where is Liza? I see Major and Mrs. Grierley and

I assume that is poor Duke on the bench, but where is Liza?"

Edward's mouth was set in a grim line. "I do not know. Put her on the bench, Gavin, and let us see if we can make some sense of this."

Carina had clutched instinctively at Gavin's arm as he lowered her to the bench. He patted her hand comfortingly and straightened up, flexing his stiff arms. Mrs. Grierley plumped herself down beside Carina, putting a consoling arm about the young girl's shoulders.

"Are you quite unhurt, child?"

"Yes, thank you, Mrs. Grierley, but what has happened to Liza?" Carina gazed imploringly at Edward, but it was Gavin who answered:

"We can as yet be sure of nothing, but let us detail what we do know. You, Ned, received a message purporting to be from me which took you away from the Grierleys and Elizabeth. At about the same time or a bit before, Carina and Pevency here wandered away from the others." He looked up for Edward's nod. "Elizabeth was briefly drawn apart from the Grierleys by Lady Moreton who is certainly above suspicion. She began to follow the Grierleys but never caught up with them. Within a moment or two they checked on her progress but she was nowhere to be seen. Is this essentially correct?" Both Grierleys signified assent and Gavin continued more slowly. "Meanwhile in another location, right here to be precise, Pevency and Carina paused at this bench and Pevency was knocked out by a blow from behind." He ignored Lord Pevency's startled exclamation, looking instead at Carina for confirmation.

"Yes, a man hit Duke and then grabbed me and

carried me to the little summerhouse at the end of this alley. He tied my hands and feet and put something across my mouth so I could not call out, then just left. I do not know how long it was before Gavin found me. It seemed an eternity but perhaps it was not actually so very long?" She raised her brows questioningly.

Edward was frowning in concentration. "You are implying that there is some connection between Elizabeth's disappearance and Carina's abduction? I do not quite see how."

"You have forgotten the false message removing you from the scene," inserted Gavin smoothly. "Carina and her escort were forcibly detained and the Grierleys were separated from Elizabeth briefly, just long enough for someone to entice or remove Elizabeth from the vicinity of all her friends."

"But why?" blurted Carina.

"It is possible, of course, but highly unlikely," demurred the major. "The timing for one thing is so intricate and there were five people, after all, to account for. This argues a great degree of premeditation."

"I quite agree," said Gavin, "but if not this then how does one account for a wanton attack on Pevency and Carina and a false message to Ned, purporting to be from myself specifically?" He frowned. "Who would even know that I was to be here tonight?"

The others looked at him blankly.

"I knew; Elizabeth had mentioned it," Edward said slowly, "but I am at a complete loss to suggest anyone else who might have known. And we are forgetting the person who attacked Pevency and abducted Carina was presumably a stranger who could not have known we would be here tonight."

"But it was not a stranger!" cried Carina excitedly.

All eyes turned to the pale young girl who now sat bolt upright on the bench.

"He tried very hard to prevent my getting a glimpse of him but I did, and I recognized him. Gavin, do you remember the highwayman who held up our chaise a couple of months ago? He had a long scar from his nose down past the left side of his mouth and so did the man who struck Duke. I did not hear his voice tonight but I could not be mistaken about that scar." Her voice flattened again. "But why should he do such a thing—revenge?"

"Good God!" exploded Gavin, and everyone's attention switched from Carina to him but his eyes were on Edward alone. "Ned, I saw this man Carina has just described at Figg's two nights ago in company with Edgemere. Money changed hands and I thought then that Edgemere had some dashed queer friends."

Carina's eyes had followed Gavin's to Edward and what she saw in his face shocked her profoundly. Never had she witnessed such a flame of sheer rage flicker across anyone's countenance, to be replaced instantly by a deadly calm. He looked entirely capable of murder, but his words were quiet.

"Well, now we know who and why. Only the where remains to be discovered. Gavin, you check the water entrance and I'll try to find out if his coach was noticed at the carriage entrance. She was wearing white tonight," he called over his shoulder.

The two men were gone before the rest of the party could draw a breath.

"I do not understand." Mrs. Grierley turned to the young girl sitting so very still, a deathly pallor rendering her frighteningly fragile. Hastily she put her plump arm around Carina's shoulders and, feeling her trembling, rocked her soothingly as one would a very young child. After a moment Carina drew a shuddering breath, then sat up straight again. No one had spoken, but Lord Pevency had taken her hand.

"I am all right now, ma'am." She half smiled at the young man and gently withdrew her hand. "Edward and Gavin believe Lord Edgemere has abducted Liza. You see he offered for her recently and was quite put out by her refusal."

"It's no secret that Edgemere's all to pieces, of course," the major said, "but, damn, to abduct a bride in this day and age—no, it's unthinkable."

"Then where is Liza, Major Grierley? And why should a highwayman who had accepted money from Lord Edgemere two nights ago hit Duke on the head and remove me from the scene? Edward was also made to leave her side by a trick. After that it was not such a difficult thing surely to seize an instant when Liza might be detached from her friends."

"But surely your sister would not willingly go anywhere with Edgemere?" Lord Pevency put in frowningly.

"Of course not, but there had already been one false message delivered. Perhaps Lord Edgemere had another one sent to Liza to draw her away to an area where he might seize her."

"Here comes Delawney," said Major Grierley.

Carina looked up hopefully but Gavin had no information. Edward, approaching swiftly, had another tale to tell, however.

"They left by coach about forty-five mintues ago. The carriage had no identifying crest but the postilions had been talking while they waited and the descriptions fit. They were not expecting to drive all night and they headed back toward the bridge. That means he doesn't plan to take her to Edgemere Castle, at least not tonight. It is along the Brighton Road," he explained, noting Carina's puzzled expression. He rubbed one hand along the back of his neck absently, a habit of his when thinking deeply, then exploded, "Where in God's name can he be taking her?"

Gavin, who had been gnawing his bottom lip thoughtfully during this explanation, now spoke slowly: "Edgemere has a small place near Windsor, just a few miles from my brother-in-law's estate. It is quite notorious in fact—he brings parties down for weekend revels that have provided the choicest bits of scandal in the area for the past several years. Any respectable woman visiting there would be ruined."

Edward made a swift decision, "It is already past one A.M. I am not likely to find any more precise information tonight. I must gamble that you are correct and go after them at once. Will you see Carina safely home, Tom?" he asked the major.

"I'll do that," Gavin offered quickly. "Ned, you'll make better time if you take my curricle from here even though I have only a pair. I presume he had a team?"

"Yes, but I'll take your grays over any team I could hire at this hour. Many thanks." He had turned away, then came back to Carina. "I'll find her, my dear, tonight if possible, but I swear to you, he'll never make her wed him in any case. England is not large enough to hide him from me."

Carina valiantly attempted a smile, but fear lurked in the gray depths as she watched Edward disappear down the path accompanied by Gavin who was giving him more precise directions.

"Take Finkston with you; you may want him to send a message. He has a pistol. Are you well blunted?"

"Yes, no problem there."

"When you find her, Ned, bring her to my sister. We'll put a notice in the *Gazette* that she is visiting Lady Melton. I'll collect her gear from Green Street and bring it down. With luck we will come out of this unscathed." He hesitated briefly and shot a look at the steely-faced man climbing into the curricle. "Don't make it a hanging offense, Ned."

The other laughed shortly. "Have no fear, I shan't kill him, but if he lays a hand on her he will wish himself dead when I finish with him."

Gavin watched the curricle's departure with a heavy frown before returning to collect Carina and the quiet remains of the erstwhile gay party.

They took sculls to Westminster, but this time Carina was completely impervious to the still beauty of the night and the silver-streaked river. Except to say good night to the Grierleys who had offered to see Lord Pevency home since his head was giving him considerable pain, she did not speak on the return trip until the hackney carriage was approaching Green Street. Gavin too had been immersed in his own worrying speculations, but now he smiled at her and took her hand in a warm, comforting clasp which called forth a wan smile. She looked so little and forlorn but not one tear had escaped the overbright eyes during the entire ordeal of physical assault, abandonment and the cruel aftermath of fear for Elizabeth. A fierce wave of pride in her courage rose in him and it needed all his resolution to prevent himself from gathering her into his arms then and there. After this episode was resolved he would storm her defenses, but for the moment she was in dire need of comfort and rest.

"Ned will find her, little one. Try to set your mind at ease. You must sleep; I am persuaded your head is throbbing by now."

"Yes, but, oh, Gavin, suppose he—the earl I mean—does *not* take her to this weekend house of his?"

"Of course he will. You heard Ned. The postilions were not prepared for a long journey. Remember, Edgemere does not know we are aware he is responsible for Elizabeth's disappearance. Not one of us saw him tonight and he could not know you should recognize your assailant. It was sheer misfortune for him that I was at Figg's the other night. Edward will catch them before morning and bring Elizabeth to my sister's place. We shall contrive to avert any scandal. Believe that, my dear."

"Yes, if they are indeed headed for that house.

But, Gavin, I have a horrible fear that this may not be so. Lord Edgemere has a small yacht, *The Tempest*, in the river near Windsor. He is very fond of sailing; indeed, it is a passion with him. Suppose he should carry her there? Edward would never find her, at least not tonight." Now her hand clutched his imploringly and the gray eyes were raised in mute appeal.

Gavin hastened to reassure her. "It is not at all likely, Carina. The house is always ready for guests. There are servants there, but a boat is a different proposition entirely. I am convinced he has taken her to his house."

Carina sighed. "No doubt you are correct. I am so worried I cannot think straight. Thank you for bringing me home, Gavin. Good night.

It was with the deepest reluctance and an actual physical ache that Gavin watched Carina slowly enter the house. Her superb composure in the presence of the fear plainly revealed in those rainwater eyes fired him with a savage desire to wreck personal vengeance on the one who had caused her distress. Now for the first time he bitterly regretted his uncontrolled actions that had resulted in the barrier that presently existed between them. If he had acted differently on that ill-fated evening, he might now possess the right to offer her the comfort of his arms, instead of being condemned merely to witness her desolation. Had he not destroyed their former friendly relationship she might at least have turned as naturally to him as to a brother for consolation. The ride in the hackney had been an agony of restraint and now, as he entered his house, a mood of somber restlessness was overtaking him. Waiting around for news that was as likely to prove catastrophic as favorable was an utterly damnable position to be in and completely alien to his nature. It rankled that he had been unable to assist Carina in any meaningful sense. It was she who had to face the butler and her abigail with some tale of Elizabeth, and on her slim shoulders alone was placed the burden of breaking the news of the abduction to Miss Silverdown in the morning.

He paced irritably about his library, carrying a brandy glass, but his unpleasant thoughts seemed to occupy him to the exclusion of any accompanying action and the liquid remained at the same level for many moments. Behind his frowning countenance he was seeing Carina's face as she had gazed at him pleadingly just before leaving the cab. Not for a moment did he credit her premonition that Edgemere might have taken Elizabeth aboard his yacht, but *she* did, and doubtless this fear would contribute to her unease and distress on this interminable night. He balled his hand into a fist and punched viciously at an inoffensive chair that blocked his erratic path, but this small action gave no relief to the burning restlessness building up in his breast. Suddenly he came to a decision, abruptly ceasing the mad pacing. He drained his glass and hurriedly left the room, calling for his valet.

If that worthy gentleman was surprised to receive commands to produce buckskin and Hessians and send a message to the stables for a horse at nearly 2:00 A.M., he concealed it and any other emotion behind a wooden manner as he proceeded to carry out his master's instructions in every detail. Despite his intense preoccupation Gavin was touched by this quiet efficiency and tossed his man a grateful smile as he left the room a bare twenty minutes later.

"Expect me when you see me, Dewers."

CHAPTER 15

Gazing wearily and sightlessly out of the window at the silvered greenery flying past, Elizabeth wondered how long they had been driving at this mad pace. It seemed hours but she realized that the nervous strain of trying to appear calm and controlled probably contributed to this hopeless sense of having driven beyond the confines of her everyday life. She had no slightest guess as to the direction in which they were heading beyond knowing that they had recrossed the river at the beginning of the journey. Nothing looked familiar in the moon-dazzled landscape. Sternly she repressed the need to sit back and allow her taut body to relax against the velvet squabs. Instinctively she refused to be lulled into the merest semblance of normalcy. And only by concentrating fiercely on maintaining an erect posture could she keep the threatened tears of weakness and fatigue at bay.

Except to inquire for her comfort at occasional intervals, the earl sat completely silent and seemingly relaxed in the opposite corner. With a vindictiveness totally alien to her nature, Elizabeth hoped passionately that his unconcerned pose was as false as her own composure. She felt she had shaken his confidence in the outcome of his scheme at least temporarily, and resolved to win any future war of nerves.

Thus when the chaise lurched around a sharp bend and came to a noisy halt, she allowed no sign of interest or concern to escape her except for the spasmodic clasping together of her hands in her lap.

Uttering an angry protest, the earl wrenched open the door and jumped from the carriage. As the door slammed shut behind him, Elizabeth sank back against the squabs, savoring the unlooked-for solitude. She put her face in her trembling hands for a moment, trying desperately to relax enough to permit the tension to drain from her weary body. She was partially successful as long as she could keep her mind blank. Thinking accomplished nothing beyond the accentuation of her hopeless situation. She had already gleaned that the earl must have laid careful plans for tonight's abduction. She had not caught a glimpse of him at Vauxhall until the moment he appeared behind her on the path. She had noticed no familiar faces during the short time before getting into his carriage—nobody to tell Edward with whom she had left. Even the manner of their going had been unremarkable; she had left quite willingly. She pressed a shaking hand against her eyes. What must Carina and Edward be thinking by this time? She could not hope for rescue; they would have no slightest clue to help trace her. She herself had no idea where she was but it was quite clear that she must effect her own rescue.

It suddenly occurred to her that she had been wasting precious minutes in self-pity. Here was a heaven-sent opportunity to elude the earl. She peered out of the window and saw him in conversation with the coachman. There was nothing about her surroundings to tell her where she was but it appeared to be a good-sized road and must lead somewhere. If she could but hide amongst the bushes until they tired of looking for her, she would follow it till she reached some hamlet or house where she might obtain assistance in returning to London. Fortunately the night was unseasonably balmy. Her silk stole would be enough protection for a few hours. She frowned down at her white gown. It could not have been more visible but there was no help for that.

Her hand was on the off-side door when the earl reopened the other one. She spun around, her hand falling to her side, her cheeks suffused with guilty color.

The earl smiled and there was nothing reassuring in the gesture. "Has the delay seemed long to you, my dear?" he asked smoothly. "Since you seem eager to stretch your legs, you will not be put out of countenance when I tell you that, thanks to a broken trace, we shall have to walk the rest of the way. It is less than a mile however and the road surface is good. Come along."

Perforce she must take his hand and allow him to assist her down from the carriage. A scene would avail her nothing and she needed her strength to form another plan of escape. Silently she descended and they began to walk. Strangely enough now, the earl became rather expansive. As they trudged along the deserted road, he sought to ease her fears as to where she was being taken.

"It is a small house but quite comfortable, my

dear. The servants will have everything in readiness for your little visit. They are very reliable and, provided you do not try to leave my hospitality unexpectedly, completely at your service."

Elizabeth ignored the warning in this and asked quietly, "How long do you intend to keep me here?"

"That is for you to say, Elizabeth. I have a special license in my pocket. You may return to town as soon after our wedding as it may please you to do."

At this Elizabeth stumbled and had to be steadied by the earl's hand under her elbow. He did not remove it after she regained her footing and some instinct warned her to control the shrinking she felt at his touch. At the moment he was at his most urbane, but she knew his sadistic nature would enjoy forcing her submission to his demands. That he was enjoying himself at this moment was apparent, all earlier qualms about her eventual capitulation soothed by the distance they had come and her own seeming acceptance of the situation, at least physically.

Presently they turned down a short lane that eventually ended at the drive to a charming, small, brick residence of fairly recent date nestled amongst a shrubbery that must have drawn exclamations from Elizabeth under other circumstances. The uncomfortable walk in flimsy sandals, however, had removed any fighting spirit remaining after the long ordeal that had begun as a merry evening for six congenial people. By now Elizabeth was so completely fatigued as to be almost grateful for the support of the earl's arm as he ushered her ceremoniously into his house.

The expressionless butler was obviously expecting them and he led the way to a small sitting room where a table was set for a late supper. Although the night had not been cold she gratefully noted the cheerful fire crackling in the fireplace. She was in a state of numb misery, and for the first time a new and disconcerting element of embarrassment was present. Before she had been too dismayed and angry to consider this aspect of her plight, but now she had to force herself not to avoid the impersonal glance of the gray-haired butler as he seated her. Her spirit cringed at the picture she must present, arriving in the middle of the night in evening dress unaccompanied by a maid and unencumbered by so much as a bandbox, or even a toothbrush for that matter. She tried to subdue the heat rising in her cheeks, knowing she had yet to face an abigail and perhaps even the housekeeper. A wave of revulsion rose in her as she glanced at the attractively laid table. The thought of food was repulsive, and when the obsequious butler had at last left the room, she desperately cut into the earl's bland description of his cook's special way with ham and artichokes as he pressed her to try some.

"Please, my lord, I wish nothing to eat. I am exceedingly fatigued. Have I your permission to retire?" She gazed at him imploringly.

"Naturally you must please yourself about eating, my dear—I would not dream of pressing you, but you really cannot retire until we have at least drunk to our prospective union." He smiled as he proceeded to fill two glasses from a bottle of champagne at his elbow, and Elizabeth, watching his attractive mouth take on an amiable curve totally belied by those cold eyes, shivered and thought despairingly that he must have enjoyed pulling the wings off insects as a boy. The cruel satisfaction he derived from the suffering of others frightened her but she dropped her lashes to conceal this as he handed her one of the glasses and pronounced a glib toast. Stubbornly she kept her eyes and her glass on the table, and after a pregnant instant his voice came softly but with an unmistakably threatening edge. "Come, my dear, you are not drinking. I must insist. It will relax you and help you to sleep better in a strange house."

Elizabeth had resolved to win all battles of nerves. She sensed that here was the first skirmish and, steeling herself, raised her glance to his implacably smiling face.

"I wish nothing to eat or drink, my lord," she said quietly. "Will you please call someone to show me to my room?"

The blue eyes met his cold amber gaze unflinchingly for perhaps five seconds, but the outcome of this clash of wills was not to be known, for into the tense silence came a sudden loud banging on the front door, followed shortly by sounds of an altercation in the hall. The earl's fingers had tightened about his wineglass and Elizabeth hoped the emotion flashing across his face for an unguarded instant was fear. She scarcely breathed as hope rose unbidden, and her silent prayers were answered as the scuffle in the hall ceased abruptly and the door to the small apartment was flung open. For the briefest of seconds she clearly glimpsed Edward's beloved countenance before her eyes misted with nervous tears.

The earl had surged to his feet with an angry snarl as the door opened, but to Elizabeth's excited fancy everything stood still for an eternity while Edward's hard, anxious expression slowly relaxed as he reassured himself of her safety. He spoke evenly:

"Gavin's curricle is at the end of the drive. Finkston is there and will assist you. I will join you shortly." He stood back from the door, waiting for her to leave, not even glancing at the other man after the first assessing look. Elizabeth closed her lips on whatever protest she had been about to utter, contenting herself with an urgent whisper as she obediently left the room. "Please take care, Edward."

She glanced rather nervously around the hall as she hurried toward the main door, unsure what she would do if anyone attempted to prevent her leaving. The butler was sprawled on his hands and knees, his whole attention riveted on testing the condition of his jaw and he did not so much as glance her way as she opened the door and slipped out in one swift movement. She sped down the drive to where Finkston awaited her. He had already turned the curricle and reached down a hand to help her. He evidenced no surprise at her appearance, and she was grateful to be spared the necessity for explanations. She realized she was trembling as if with ague, but the resultant self-disgust did not enable her to control her betraying limbs. She was not aware that even this shame at her weakness was the result of the accumulated stresses of a nightmarish evening and the abrupt cessation of her need for self-discipline signaled by Edward's miraculous arrival. She feared that even Finkston's silent sympathy might cause her total collapse as she sat, shaking, peering down the drive for Edward.

When he came with long, purposeful strides it was not Elizabeth but Finkston who noted the torn cravat and the handkerchief bound around the knuckles of his left hand. In his turn, Edward, after one searching look, commanded Finkston to drive. Unmindful of the groom's enforced closeness, he gently gathered his trembling fiancée into strong arms and, murmuring soothing nothings, held her in a comforting clasp until at last the trembling stilled and she grew calm. It was heavenly peaceful in Edward's arms, but suddenly recalling the groom's presence, Elizabeth sighed and reluctantly pulled away.

"I am fine now, Edward, really. I beg your pardon for inflicting you with such a surfeit of sensibility."

"Hush, sweetheart, you are entitled to a display of screaming hysterics after this experience, but it is over now."

"That is what I find so difficult to believe. I was so sure no one would know what had happened. How did you find me?"

"It's a long story, sweetheart, better left till tomorrow when you are rested." He addressed himself to the groom. "How much farther, Finkston?"

"About a mile and a half, sir."

"Are we not going back to London, then, Edward?"

"No, my dear. We would need a change of

horses and it would be practically daybreak by the time we returned. Gavin advised me to take you to his sister's house which is quite near here."

"Where is here?"

"Not far from Windsor. What's the matter, sweetheart? You look disturbed."

"Well, this is such a terrible time to arrive at anyone's door. What will the Meltons think?"

"They are quite likely already appraised of the situation and expecting us. Gavin was to send a message by one of the grooms. In any case we shall tell them the whole truth. It will go no further."

"Oh, I do not fear gossip from the Meltons, but perhaps you have forgotten Lord Edgemere. He is just the type to enjoy spreading scandal and most likely will seek revenge."

"I have not forgotten him, but he would never dare spread a story in which he showed so poorly," Edward said grimly. "In any event, for the next few weeks he will be unable to do much talking at all, or even eating."

"Ahh! Broken his bone box for him, have you, guv'nor?"

The immense satisfaction in the voice of the shamelessly eavesdropping Finkston caused Elizabeth to go off in peals of delighted mirth. To Edward the bell chimes of her laughter were far more beautiful than any of the music he had heard that night. He had been so afraid of the effect of such a nightmarish adventure on a sensitive girl like Elizabeth, but it seemed he had made the common error of judging her character solely by her delicate beauty. The smile that so warmed his austere features were beginning to glow deep in his eyes as he gazed at his lovely girl's suddenly sparkling face, and he whispered thankfully,

"Yes, it is indeed over now."

Elizabeth slipped her hand into his and, resting her tired head against the welcoming shoulder, closed her eyes in contentment as they continued to drive on.

CHAPTER 16

The moon had been partially veiled by a persistent scrap of cloud for the last few minutes and Gavin had slowed the big black to a careful walk. He was very tired now and impatient for his bed, but still glad he had come on this wild-goose chase. The message in Carina's eyes had been unmistakable, and he could not have faced her with a clear conscience had he not obeyed the silent plea. As expected, the yacht, *Tempest*, when he found it after some floundering, had proved to be deserted. Gavin would not have been surprised to discover the earl had had to sell his pretty toy; he must be even deeper in the river Tick than was common knowledge to have resorted to this desperate abduction. He refused to consider the possibility that Edward might not have caught up with them yet as he urged the horse forward at a faster pace. Bella's place was just a couple of miles ahead now. He was practically certain he'd find Edward and Elizabeth there, but it would be an enormous relief to be assured his hunch had proved correct.

His attention returned from his troublesome thoughts to Thunderer who was acting strangely. His head was up and he appeared to be listening for something. At first Gavin heard nothing but the usual night rustlings that had accompanied him for the better part of this tiresome ride, then he stiffened as he caught the unmistakable sound of a horse's soft whinny. Thunderer responded in kind. Knowing honest men were unlikely to be abroad at this hour, Gavin brought out a pistol and kept it at the ready as he let the black have his way. Around the next bend in the lane he halted abruptly, staring in amazement at the small figure seated beneath a big elm. A boy! Gavin frowned in puzzlement. What was such a young lad doing abroad at this hour and sitting under a tree as though he had all the time in the world? As he approached, the answer to one at least of the questions buzzing round in his head became apparent. The boy had evidently sustained an injury of some sort, for he was holding his ankle with one hand though his eyes never left the rider emerging from the darkness of a more heavily wooded area.

Something about the stiff little figure looked vaguely familiar. A warning shock of awareness ran along Gavin's nerves as, eyes narrowed, he decreased the distance between them. Suddenly the small figure let out a gasp and almost at the same instant Gavin froze in the saddle. It could not be! For a further fractional second his astounded brain refused to heed the evidence of his eyes. Even Carina would not be so heedless as to don boy's clothing and venture unescorted upon such an errand as this in the small hours of the morning.

"Gavin! Oh, thank God, you are the answer to a prayer!"

The glad cry banished all hope that his eyes had deceived him. He stared into the upturned face of the girl he loved, unable to trust himself to speak for a moment as he struggled to subdue a wave of mingled rage and fear at her foolishness. Wordlessly he descended from his horse who picked his way across exposed tree roots to join another horse standing quietly a few yards away. To some extent his feelings mastered him and Carina's eager look faded as he seized her roughly by the shoulders and administered a slight but unmistakable shake.

"Carina, I could strangle you for this." The words were uttered with a kind of controlled desperation, but the suggestion of clenched teeth and glittering eye proved the last straw for Carina. If he had ranted at her in his usual style, she might have rallied to her own defense, but now her face crumpled and two huge tears formed, trembled on the edge of her lashes, then spilled silently over and ran down her cheeks, to be followed by their successors.

"Oh, lord, child, I am sorry. Don't cry . . ." Gavin paused helplessly. Never had he seen the intrepid Carina at a loss in a situation and he was unsure of how to handle the child. But this was not the abandoned weeping of a hurt child, he realized almost at once. This was a woman, worried, unhappy, completely fatigued and at the end of her strength, releasing the inevitable tears of emotional weakness. Wordlessly he pulled her close and with a shuddering sigh she relaxed against him. For a moment he simply held her thankfully, then reluctantly he pushed her a fraction away and looked down into her face.

"Listen, Carina, this is no place to talk. I must get you to my sister's. Are you hurt? Why were you sitting under that tree?"

"My horse stumbled and I took a toss. It was my own fault; I was not attending. Were you looking for *The Tempest* too?"

"Yes. It was deserted. You might have known I would obey such an urgent though unspoken request, Carina. Look at me."

She hung her head, unable to meet his demanding eyes. He put his hand under her chin and forced her to meet his serious glance. "You must know I would do anything for you. This," indicating her boy's garb with an outflung hand, "was totally unnecessary."

"I . . . I did not know. How could I?" Hastily she avoided his challenging gaze and went on hurriedly, "I did not mean for you to go, and anyway, you did not think they might have gone there, but I could not rest easy so I . . . I decided I must go myself. Can you not understand how I felt?"

Gavin's stern expression softened as he met her pleading, tear-drenched eyes. "Yes," he sighed, "I suppose I do, but I also understand that you need a guardian and, by heaven, you are going to acquire one just as soon as it can be arranged, for my peace of mind's sake . . . and other reasons," he finished softly as, blushing hotly, she pulled out of his arms.

"Never the time or the place," he murmured ruefully. "Can you ride?" At her nod he whistled the horses over and helped her to mount. "We shall have to go slowly for a bit till we come out of these trees. Will you tell me how you managed to get here by yourself?"

She watched him remount the patient Thunderer while she marshaled her thoughts. They were able to walk together on the path.

"I do not know exactly when I decided to come. After you left I went inside and told Coleman Elizabeth had gone on a visit to your sister quite unexpectedly because Lady Melton had taken ill and needed her assistance on the return trip. I said I would bring Elizabeth's clothes down tomorrow. When I got to my room, however, I simply could not go to bed. How could I sleep? I could not forget about that wretched boat either, so I made up my mind to try to find it." At his impatient exclamation she said defensively, "Well, if they *had* gone there Edward would not have been able to find her, but if I arrived, he, the earl, I mean, could not compromise her. Having her sister with her would answer better than having a maid."

"Never mind all that. Where did you get those clothes in the middle of the night?"

"I had them. They were the ones I wore when I . . ." She faltered and he finished for her: "I remember, when you witnessed that mill."

"Yes. Abby had packed them away but she remembered where they were and got them for me." She noted his quick frown.

"You told your maid?"

"I trust Abby implicitly. I needed her help to get out of the house unnoticed and to hire this horse. Also to find these clothes, as I said. I thought I would be safer dressed this way at night."

"Yes," he admitted. "That was the one intelligent thing you did. If you had to be misguided enough to attempt such an insane adventure, you would do better as a boy."

"Besides, I enjoy riding astride," confessed Carina impishly. "In fact, if it were not for the worry about Liza, this would be a splendid adventure. It is a warm, beautiful night, the moon is bright and gives everything a different aspect—the trees and the roadway look entirely different. I felt like the last person in the world. It really was rather splendid."

Gavin groaned. Here was the old Carina with a vengeance. With a very successful season behind her, at least one offer apart from his own if Ned was correct, and another imminent judging from the look in young Pevency's eyes, and she still sounded like the child who was disappointed not to capture a highwayman. She would never change, and finally he came to the somewhat startling conclusion, in view of his own efforts to convert her into a typical debutante, that he did not want her to change in any slightest particular. He shook his head dazedly as he reached this momentous realization. Idiot that he had been! He loved her gay irreverence, her sense of adventure and great companionability. Her beauty pleased him, but it was the unquenchable spirit of the girl that he loved with every fiber of his being.

They had come to a more open area finally and were able to set a faster pace. Carina was tiring now, and as the distance diminished to their destination she fell silent. Gavin knew she was desperately afraid she might not find Elizabeth at the end of this ride, but there was nothing he could do except get her to Bella's place as quickly as humanly possible.

At last they turned off into a tree-bordered drive. Carina turned to him mutely, but he could sense her sudden reluctance to reach the end of a journey that might prove to have been in vain. Her uncertainty and fear were his own, and he knew this was how it would be for the rest of his life.

"Don't worry, love, Ned will find her even if he has not done so as yet, but I feel certain we shall find they are here before us."

Carina nodded silently. They rode right to the front entrance where a lantern glowed. He was expected anyway, or Ned still was, he thought with sudden misgiving. The door opened at his first knock. The stately butler, no less impressive in a brown dressing gown than his formal garb, greeted him as though the arrival at 4:00 A.M. of the mistress's brother with his arm around a young girl dressed as a village youth was an every day occurence.

"Good evening, Murdstone. Has Sir Edward Lynton arrived?"

"Yes, sir, about an hour ago."

Gavin could feel Carina's tenseness as he said as casually as a pounding heart and a dry throat would allow, "Was he alone?"

"No, sir, Miss Raven accompanied him. They have both retired, sir." No hint of interest or emotion colored his precise tones. The perfect butler, Gavin thought admiringly. He was given no further time to ponder Murdstone's excellent qualities, however, for Carina suddenly sagged in his grasp and he swept her up into his arms and carried her into the small saloon off the hall.

"Get some hot milk," he ordered over his shoulder, "and send someone to show Miss Raven to her room."

Once in the cosy room he did not set the now feebly protesting girl on her feet, but sat down himself on a rose-colored settee and, keeping Carina in his arms, urged, "Cry it out, darling, you have earned it."

But it was a dry-eyed, radiant countenance that was raised temptingly to his, as once again Carina confounded him.

"Oh, thank heaven! Such a relief! Isn't Edward wonderful? Oh, I could hug him," she declared delightedly.

"Ahem, Miss Raven, might I suggest an even more worthy recipient of your embraces closer to hand?" he said in a wheedling tone, tenderly smoothing back the little lock of hair that had fallen onto her forehead.

Carina's fabulous eyelashes swept down to hide her expression as she murmured primly, "I seem to recall, sir, that you once told me quite forcefully that you did *not* yearn to push back that lock of hair. Am I to gather that you have had a change of heart?"

There was a moment's amazed silence, then Gavin let out a shout of laughter that brought two gray eyes, brimful of mischief, up to meet and kindle a fire in his.

"Why, you brass-faced little gypsy, I believe you are trying to flirt with me." His light manner changed as he gazed into those remarkable eyes looking shyly but steadily into his own. "At last," he breathed a trifle unsteadily, "Carina, we must talk. I . . ." The sound of approaching footsteps effectively quelled his rising ardor, and with a small groan he set her on her feet and rose to meet his sister's housekeeper as she bustled into the room. He took the glass from the tray she carried and watched while Carina drained it. A wave of shyness kept her eyes glued to the glass in her hand, and as she made to follow the motherly woman upstairs, he said hurriedly,

"I shall seek a private interview with you tomorrow, Miss Raven, to continue our conversation."

Carina blushed at the housekeeper's knowing look and answered with equal formality, "Of course, sir, whenever it is convenient. I'll bid you good night." Sternly she repressed a strong impulse to look back at him as she followed the ample figure up to a charming room, though she was in no condition to appreciate this pleasant fact. Buoyed up by excitement for so long, tiredness suddenly hit her like a blow. She stumbled entering the room.

The housekeeper clucked dispprovingly. "Poor child, you are asleep on your feet and small wonder at this hour. Come over here and sit. I'll get you ready for bed."

"But I have no clothes," Carina protested, close to tears of pure fatigue by this time.

"When we heard about the other young lady coming—that would be your sister, would it?—her ladyship laid out some of her own night things. Now you never mind thinking; just turn while I undo those buttons, there's a lamb."

Numbly Carina allowed herself to be prepared

for bed by the kindly housekeeper who kept up a continuous flow of chatter, none of which required answers or concentration which was fortunate because Carina was beyond either skill. Mrs. Hackley nobly contained whatever normal curiosity she might have felt at the strange parade of unexpected guests, and within ten minutes Carina had tumbled into a most welcome bed and into unconsciousness.

Someone must have pulled back the draperies because sunlight was streaming in through two large windows when Carina finally emerged from a surprisingly dreamless sleep. She yawned and stretched luxuriously after her first startled glance around the strange room, remembering clearly the momentous events of the last twenty-four hours. A rosy hue overspread her cheeks as her first coherent thoughts of the morning were identical with the last before sleep had robbed her of the pleasure they produced. She hugged to herself the memory of Gavin's expression when he had looked at her just before the housekeeper's intervention and his words promising a private conversation this morning. This morning! Why was she lying in this bed when it was perfectly obvious by the angle of the sun's rays that the morning was already well advanced? She was on the point of leaping out of bed when a soft tap on the door was followed quickly by the entrance of a smiling young maid carrying chocolate on a small tray. Immediately behind her appeared Elizabeth, also smiling.

"Liza!" shrieked Carina as she dashed across the room and threw herself at her sister who returned her embrace happily.

"Good morning, Dearest. When we looked in an hour ago, you were still sleeping deeply, so everyone agreed to allow you as much rest as you needed." She held her sister away from her and observed her closely, smiling a little at the revealing yellow nightdress that proclaimed itself part of a trousseau. "No need to ask how you are feeling after your adventure; you look blooming. Better hop back into bed for a moment and drink your chocolate. It is nearly noon, you know, so this is all you may have till luncheon."

Carina obeyed mechanically, a sudden frown crossing her brow. "Liza, I just remembered, I have no clothes. I'll not be able to join you for lunch."

Elizabeth sat on the side of the bed, watching her sister sip the chocolate. "Your things arrived an hour ago, Dearest, with Aunt Augusta. Oh, yes," she added cheerfully, noting Carina's surprise. "Messages were flying between here and town in the early hours of the morning. Poor Aunt had no notion of last night's events, or that she had temporarily lost both her charges, until she awoke this morning to find on her tray Gavin's letter and an invitation from Lady Melton to join us here for a few days. The poor dear nearly went off into hysterics when I told her the whole story backed up by Edward and Gavin's account of your part in the adventure, but she is now quite restored, thanks especially to a certain piece of information."

She stopped abruptly, and Carina was mystified by the sly smile trembling on her lips, but before she could question her, there was another tap on the door and Lady Melton entered looking as fresh as a morning glory despite her disturbed night. She was wearing pale green muslin and a smugly satisfied expression. After responding to her affectionate greeting, Carina glanced from one to the other of her attendants in bewilderment.

"Why are you both staring at me as if . . . as if you know something I do not? Oh . . .!" she broke off, blushing hotly, and both girls laughed delightedly.

Lady Melton said briskly, "Lunch will be served at one, but before that I believe you have an appointment with my very impatient brother. May I just say that I am delighted to be gaining a sister, and the very one I had picked out for Gavin?"

Carina smiled shyly. "Thank you so much." She turned to her sister with a slightly anxious air. "Liza, do you approve?"

"Goose! Of course, I approve. I picked out Gavin for you long before Isabella selected you for him. Also Aunt Augusta is ecstatic, that is, when she forgets to be worried about a scandal developing from last night's wanderings."

"That reminds me. What about the Grierleys? They were very worried about you, and Lord Pevency too."

"Gavin saw to everything. He has been up since dawn dispatching messengers and arranging for wardrobes to be delivered. Now be a good girl and hurry and dress. He has been waiting for you for hours."

"Yes," agreed Lady Melton. "It is time you put the poor boy out of his misery."

"What shall I wear?" Carina uttered the eternal cry of womankind, and the three young women held a conference over the contents of the trunk delivered by Miss Silverdown. With two pairs of willing hands to assist, she was speedily arrayed in a filmy white muslin over a deep yellow slip decorated with matching ribbons. Elizabeth brushed the glorious red curls till they shone with sparks of gold, and Lady Melton dashed from the room, returning with a lovely spray of yellow silk roses for her dress to add the perfect touch to the charming picture Carina presented.

"Where is everyone?" she asked, rather breathless from the eager ministrations of her two loving handmaidens.

"Edward is riding over the estate with Lord Melton and Aunt Augusta is resting in her room till lunch," replied Elizabeth.

"And Gavin is awaiting your ladyship in the small saloon," reminded Lady Melton, twinkling mischievously. "He claims Mrs. Hackley interrupted a very important conversation there last night—or this morning rather—and he is eager to resume it."

"Yes, go!" ordered the laughing Elizabeth, giving her sister a little push toward the door. "He won't eat you."

Carina chuckled and ran lightly down the stairs, but her steps slowed as her confidence seeped slowly away. The door to the small saloon was open and she paused silently in the entranceway, allowing herself a few seconds pleasurable study of her lover before he became aware of her presence. She thought proudly that Gavin was a man to gladden a woman's eyes. He stood looking out of the window, lean and straight, with an erect carriage and an air of distinction in his perfectly fitting coat of olive green superfine and pale tan pantaloons. She had noted before that he always managed to appear perfectly turned out without ever giving the impression of dandyism. There was a leashed restlessness in his bearing at times that delineated his immense vitality. Now as she stood in the doorway, he removed his hand from his pocket and passed it swiftly over his dark red head before spinning abruptly around to catch her staring. She colored faintly at the look that leaped into the bright blue eyes and remained as if glued to the spot.

"Miss Carina Raven is never shy," he murmured provocatively and laughed as her chin went up. "Come here," he ordered, holding out his hand.

Obediently she glided forward and placed her hand in his, smiling up at him with shining eyes.

"Do not look at me like that or I shall kiss you, and there is much to be said first." A tender smile touched his mouth as her lashes swept down, making black curves on her creamy skin, and his grip tightened when she would have moved away in confusion.

"You deserve a poetic and eloquent proposal after the last one," he said soberly, "but I am not a poet, though I love you with a poet's passion. Will you marry me, Carina?"

"Yes," she whispered, still with eyes downcast, "if Papa agrees."

"I wrote to your father the day after the Lethbridge entertainment requesting permission to pay my addresses to you and I received his reply two days ago."

That brought her startled glance back to his, now rather amused. "What did Papa say?"

He laughed softly. "I thought you were never going to look at me again. He wished me luck and indicated his approval of the match." Looking hungrily at the glowing girl only an arm's length away, his face grew serious again. "I owe you an apology for my actions in the book room, Carina. I had been trying to get a few words with you myself all that evening, and when I saw you kissing Mercer I simply exploded with fury. I feared I had stupidly taken too long to realize that what I felt for you was not brotherly affection, but there was no excuse for the things I said. Do you forgive me?"

"Yes, of course." She looked at him rather pleadingly. "I . . . I was feeling very sorry for Tony at that moment. I suppose I meant to comfort him—it was simply an impulse."

"Had he offered for you, then?"

"Yes."

"Well, there is one thing I still believe. If you can kiss an unsuccessful candidate for your hand, why should I be left out? Come closer."

Now the color flamed into her cheeks but she could not have moved to save her life. Helplessly she stared at him as if hypnotized, but Gavin was adamant.

"Come here, Carina," he said softly, compellingly, but he made no move to assist her.

Their eyes were locked together for what seemed like a timeless eternity, and in a detached way Carina could almost witness her independent spirit melting away under his compelling gaze. At last with a shuddering little breath she surrendered completely. Swaying forward she put her hands on the lapels of his coat and placed her lips fleetingly on his. With an exultant laugh he crushed her in his arms and his mouth possessed hers in a manner she had once known and had not forgotten. This time she responded joyfully and would have been content to stay in his arms forever had not Gavin suddenly raised his head and addressed someone who had entered the room.

"You do have a fondness for playing scenes a second time, Ned," he said dryly, keeping the blushing Carina in the circle of one arm.

"So it would seem," replied Sir Edward Lynton with his customary coolness, not a whit embarrassed by the tableau he had interrupted, "but for your sake, dear boy, I do hope Carina has *not.*" Smiling benignly at the happy pair he quietly left the room.

"Well, my little love," inquired Gavin, turning to her with a quizzical smile, "are you going to slap my face this time?"

Carina said nothing, but the love shining in her eyes was enough to light a corresponding blaze in his. Swiftly he gathered her back into his embrace and proceeded to demonstrate his affection in a thoroughly satisfying manner.

Have you read these Candlelight editions from Dell?

Dell Bestsellers

- ☐ **THE USERS** by Joyce Haber $2.25 (19264-1)
- ☐ **THE HITE REPORT** by Shere Hite $2.75 (13690-3)
- ☐ **THE BOYS FROM BRAZIL** by Ira Levin $2.25 (10760-1)
- ☐ **MARATHON MAN** by William Goldman $1.95 (15502-9)
- ☐ **THE OTHER SIDE OF MIDNIGHT**
  by Sidney Sheldon $1.95 (16067-7)
- ☐ **THE GEMINI CONTENDERS**
  by Robert Ludlum $2.25 (12859-5)
- ☐ **THE RHINEMANN EXCHANGE**
  by Robert Ludlum $1.95 (15079-5)
- ☐ **SEVENTH AVENUE** by Norman Bogner........$1.95 (17810-X)
- ☐ **SUFFER THE CHILDREN** by John Saul $1.95 (18293-X)
- ☐ **RICH FRIENDS** by Jacqueline Briskin $1.95 (17380-9)
- ☐ **SLIDE** by Gerald A. Browne $1.95 (17701-4)
- ☐ **THE LONG DARK NIGHT**
  by Joseph Hayes $1.95 (14824-3)
- ☐ **THRILL** by Barbara Petty $1.95 (15295-X)
- ☐ **THE NINTH MAN** by John Lee $1.95 (16425-7)
- ☐ **THE DOGS** by Robert Calder $1.95 (12102-7)
- ☐ **NAKOA'S WOMAN** by Gayle Rogers $1.95 (17568-2)
- ☐ **FOR US THE LIVING** by Antonia Van Loon....$1.95 (12673-8)
- ☐ **ALLIGATOR** by Shelley Katz $1.95 (10167-0)
- ☐ **THE CHOIRBOYS** by Joseph Wambaugh $2.25 (11188-9)
- ☐ **SHOGUN** by James Clavell $2.75 (17800-2)
- ☐ **WHERE ARE THE CHILDREN?**
  by Mary H. Clark $1.95 (19593-4)
- ☐ **THE TURNCOAT** by Jack Lynn $1.95 (18590-4)

At your local bookstore or use this handy coupon for ordering:

Dell | **DELL BOOKS**
P.O. BOX 1000, PINEBROOK, N.J. 07058

Please send me the books I have checked above. I am enclosing $_____
(please add 35¢ per copy to cover postage and handling). Send check or money
order—no cash or C.O.D.'s. Please allow up to 8 weeks for shipment.

Mr/Mrs/Miss_____

Address_____

City_____ State/Zip_____